U0001093

美式圖解英漢辭典

附 MP3

# 小朋友自學 雙語園地

監修：陳家裕（兒童英語創意者）
編著：曹彊・Cries 校訂：Andy

萬人出版社

國家圖書館出版品預行編目(CIP)資料

小朋友自學雙語園地 ： 美式圖解英漢辭典 /
曹疆, Cries 編著. -- 初版. -- 新北市 ：
萬人, 2017.01
面 ； 公分
ISBN 978-957-461-325-0(精裝附光碟)
英語 2.字典
805.132 105020713

# 小朋友自學雙語園地

美式圖解英漢辭典

編　　著 / 曹 疆 · Cries
監　　修 / 陳家裕
校　　訂 / Andy
發 行 者 / 謝長庚
出 版 者 / 萬人出版社有限公司
地　　址 / 新北市新北產業園區五權七路 68 號 3 樓
電　　話 / 02-22980501 傳　真 / 02-22980415
郵政劃撥 / 01194105
總 經 銷 / 時報文化出版企業股份有限公司
地　　址 / 桃園市龜山區萬壽路二段 351 號
電　　話 / 02-23066842
2017 年 元月版
定　　價 / 380 元 (書附 MP3)



內政部登記政局版台業字第 1822 號
E-mail:mass.book@msa.hinet.net
www.massbook.com.tw

美式圖解英漢辭典　附MP3

# 小朋友自學雙語園地

監修：陳家裕（兒童英語創意者）
編著：曹彊・Cries　校訂：Andy

萬人出版社

國家圖書館出版品預行編目(CIP)資料

小朋友自學雙語園地 ： 美式圖解英漢辭典 /
曹疆, Cries 編著. -- 初版. -- 新北市 ：
萬人, 2017.01
面 ； 公分
ISBN 978-957-461-325-0(精裝附光碟)
英語 2.字典
805.132　　　　　　　　　　105020713

# 小朋友自學雙語園地

## 美式圖解英漢辭典

編　　著 / 曹疆 · Cries
監　　修 / 陳家裕
校　　訂 / Andy
發 行 者 / 謝長庚
出 版 者 / 萬人出版社有限公司
地　　址 / 新北市新北產業園區五權七路 68 號 3 樓
電　　話 / 02-22980501 傳 真 / 02-22980415
郵政劃撥 / 01194105
總 經 銷 / 時報文化出版企業股份有限公司
地　　址 / 桃園市龜山區萬壽路二段 351 號
電　　話 / 02-23066842
２０１７ 年 元月版
定　　價 / 380 元 （書附 MP3）

# 前　言

　　由於科技不斷進步，世界各國交流平凡，尤其我國已邁向先進國家，國際化、自由化乃理所當然。而英語是公認國際語言，將來國人若不懂英語，則寸步難行，而據語言專家表示，學習語言年齡層越小，學得越快、越自然。

　　目前政府已體認出此問題，現已規定於國小開始上英語課程。由於教育不能輸在起跑點，許多家長當小孩3歲時就找尋有關學中文、英文教材，來教導小朋友。茲為了初學者對中文、英文可快樂學習。由本人及英文專家、美籍教授編著本書，藉以提高小朋友對雙語；中文、英語的興趣及學習效果。

作　者　謹識

**a** [e,弱ə] 冠 一個

Mike has *a* banana and an apple.

邁克有一支香蕉和一個蘋果。

**an** [æn 弱,ne] 冠 一個

a,an 的用法

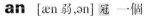

a, an 都可用在一個表示單數可數名詞之前，但 a 用在讀音以子音音標開頭的單字前，an 用在讀音以母音音標開頭的單字前。

例如：

a boy 一個男孩， a coat 一件上衣， an eye 一隻眼睛，

an orange 一個橘子

**able** ['ebl] 形 有能力的，能幹的

Billy is *able* to play football.

比利會踢足球。

**about** [ə'baʊt] 介 ①關於 ②大約

① This book is *about* Franklin.

這是一本關於富蘭克林的書。

②We left school at *about* five o'clock.

我們大約五點鐘離開學校。

**above** [ə'bʌv] 介 在……上面

The plane is flying *above* the lake.

那架飛機正在湖面上飛行。

反 below 在……之下

**accident** ['æksədənt] 名 意外的事，事故

I hit you by *accident*.

我無意中碰到了你。

## ache [ek] 動 痛

When it rains, my head *aches.*
在陰雨天氣，我的頭痛。

## across [ə'krɔs] 介 橫過，穿過

Jim is running *across* the street.
吉姆正跑過這條街道。

反 along 沿著

### act [ækt] 名 幕

My favorite *act* is scene four. 我最喜歡第四幕。

動 扮演，表演
Tom *acted* as a king in the play.
湯姆在這齣戲裏扮演了一個國王。

### actor ['æktɚ] 名 男演員

Brian is an excellent *actor.*
布萊恩是一位優秀的男演員。

## actress ['æktrɪs] 名 女演員

Sue wants to be an *actress.*
蘇想成爲一名女演員。

## add [æd] 動 增加，加

Please *add* up all your money.
請把你所有的錢加起來。

## address [ə'drɛs] 名 地址，住址

Please give me your *address* so we can keep in touch.
請把你的地址告訴我，這樣我們就可以保持聯絡了。

## advise [əd'vaɪz] 動 建議

Their teacher *advises* them to be careful.
他們的老師建議他們當心點。

## aeroplane ['ɛrə,plen,'ærəplen] (英) 名
## airplane ['ɛr,plen,'ærplen] (美) 名

飛機

We took an *airplane* to America
我們乘飛機去美國。

**afraid** [ə'fred] 形 害怕的

Don't be *afraid*.

不要害怕。

反 brave 勇敢的

**Africa** ['æfrɪkə] 名 非洲

Mr. White went to *Africa* last Sunday.

懷特先生上星期天去了非洲。

世界七大洲表示法

Asia 亞洲； Africa 非洲； North America 北美洲；

South America 南美洲； Antarctica 南極洲；

Europe 歐洲； Oceania 大洋洲

**after** ['æftɚ] 介 在……之後

*After* you leave, please close the door.

你走的時候請關上門。

反 before 在……以前

**afternoon** [,æftɚ'nun] 名 下午

Good *afternoon*, boys and girls!

孩子們，午安！

一天中時刻表示法

morning 上午； noon 中午；

afternoon 下午； evening 晚上；

night 夜晚； midnight 午夜

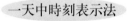

**again** [ə'gɛn, ə'gen] 副 又，再

Please say it *again*.

請再說一遍。

**against** [ə'gɛnst, ə'genst] 介 ①反對 ②靠

① No one is *against* this plan.

沒有人反對這個計劃。

② Sue is leaning *against* the tree.

蘇正倚靠在樹上。

**age** [edʒ] 名 年齡
It's impolite to ask someone's *age*.
詢問他人的年齡是不禮貌的。

**agree** [ə'grɪ] 動 同意，贊同
I *agree* with you.
我完全同意你的意見。
Rose *agreed* to help Mike with his English.
羅斯答應幫助邁克學英語。
反 disagree 不同意

**ahead** [ə'hɛd] 副 在……之前，預先
Mary is *ahead* of Bill.
瑪麗在比爾的前面。

**aim** [em] 名 目標，意圖
You have a good *aim*.
你的動機很好。

　　動 瞄準，對準
Jim is *aiming* at the bird.
吉姆正在瞄準那隻鳥。

**air** [ɛr,ær] 名 空氣
We can't live without *air*.
離開空氣，我們無法生存。

**airport** ['ɛr,port] 名 飛機場
You can see many airplanes at the *airport*.
在飛機場你能看見許多架飛機。

**alike** [ə'laɪk] 形 相同的，相似的
They look *alike*.
他們看起來相似。

**alive** [ə'laɪv] 形 活著的

The dog is still *alive*.

那隻狗仍然活著

反 dead 死的

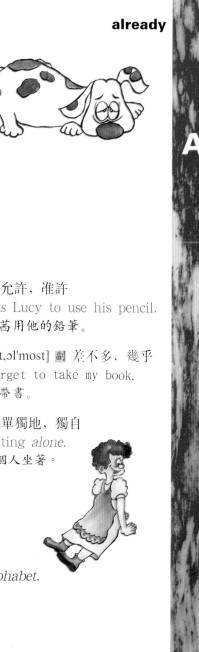

**all** [ɔl] 形 全部的，所有的

David spent *all* his money.

大衛花光了他所有的錢。

反 some 一些

代 大家，全體

We are *all* here.

我們都在這兒。

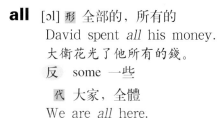

**allow** [ə'laʊ] 動 允許，准許

Peter *allows* Lucy to use his pencil.

彼得允許露茜用他的鉛筆。

**almost** ['ɔl,most,ɔl'most] 副 差不多、幾乎

I *almost* forget to take my book.

我險些忘記帶書。

**alone** [ə'lon] 副 單獨地，獨自

Helen is sitting *alone*.

海倫獨自一個人坐著。

**along** [ə'lɔŋ] 介 沿著

I like to walk *along* the river.

我喜歡沿河邊散步。

**alphabet** ['ælfə,bɛt] 名 字母表

There are 26 letters in English *alphabet*.

在英語字母表裏有26個字母。

**already** [ɔl'rɛdɪ] 副 已經

It's *already* twelve o'clock now.

現在已經十二點了。

A

**also** ['ɔlso] 副 也，並且

Mary likes swimming. Sue *also* likes swimming.

瑪麗喜歡游泳,蘇也喜歡游泳。

**A**

**always** ['ɔlwez,'ɔlwɪz] 副 總是，一直

Mr. White is *always* busy.

懷特先生總是很忙。

**a.m. A.M.** ['e'ɛm] 名 上午

Jim goes to school at 7:00 *a.m.*.

吉姆早上七點上學。

**America** [ə'mɛrəkə,ə'mɛrɪkə] 名 美國，美洲

The Smiths come from *America*.

史密斯一家來自美國。

**美國全稱**

the United States of America

簡寫爲: USA 或 US

**among** [ə'mʌŋ] 介 在……中間

Kate is hiding *among* the boxes.

凱特正藏在箱子中間。

注

among 表示"三者以上之間"，between 用於"兩者之間"。

**amuse** [ə'mjuz,ə'mɪʊz] 動 逗……樂，逗……笑

The clown *amused* the children

with his tricks.

小丑用他的把戲逗得孩子們直樂。

**and** [ɛnd,弱 ənd] 連 和，又

Lucy can speak English and French.

露茜會講英語和法語。

**angry** ['æŋgrɪ] 形 生氣的，發怒的

Diana is very *angry* at her cat.

戴安娜對她的貓非常生氣。

注

對事、物生氣時用 angry at，對人時，

通常用 angry with。

反 calm 平靜

**animal** ['ænəml̩] 名 動物

There are many *animals* at the zoo.

動物園裏有許多動物。

**ankle** ['æŋkl̩] 名 脚踝

Mike hurt his *ankle*.

邁克扭傷了他的脚踝。

**another** [ə'nʌðɚ] 形 另一的，別的

Billy wants *another* cup of coffee.

比利想再要一杯咖啡。

**answer** ['ænsɚ] 名 答案

Rose knows the right *answer*.

羅斯知道正確答案。

動 回答，答覆

Will you *answer* the telephone?

請你接一下電話好嗎?

反 ask 問

**ant** [ænt] 名 螞蟻

There were many *ants*
at our picnic place.

我們的野餐地點有許多螞蟻。

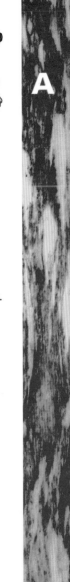

A

monkey 猴子

elephant 大象

tiger 老虎

ostrich 鴕鳥

lion 獅子

wolf 狼

rhinoceros 犀牛

leopard 豹

giraffe
長頸鹿

bear 熊

woodpecker
啄木鳥

snake
蛇

ebra 斑馬

crocodile
鱷魚

9

**any** ['ɛnɪ] 形 ①任何的 ②一些（常用於疑問句、否定句）
　　① Choose *any* book you like.
　　　你喜歡什麼書，就選什麼書。
　　② Do you have *any* food?
　　　你有一些食物嗎？

**anybody** ['ɛnɪˌbɑdɪ,'ɛnɪˌbʌdɪ] 代 任何人
　　Can *anybody* come to my party?
　　有人來出席我的晚會嗎？
　　anyone = anybody

**anything** ['ɛnɪˌθɪŋ] 代 任何事物
　　You may have *anything* on the table.
　　你可以拿桌子上的任何東西。

**appear** [ə'pɪr] 動 ①出現，顯露 ②看來（似乎）
　　① A bright star suddenly *appeared*.
　　　一顆明亮的星星突然出現了。
　　反　disappear 消失
　　② She *appears* to be crying.
　　　她看上去似乎要哭。

**apple** ['æpl] 名 蘋果
　　There is a worm in this *apple*.
　　這個蘋果裏有一條小蟲。

**April** ['eprəl,'eprɪl] 名 四月
　　It rains a lot in *April*.
　　四月份雨水很多。

**argue** ['ɑgjʊ] 動 爭論，爭辯
　　I don't want to *argue* with you.
　　我不想和你爭辯。

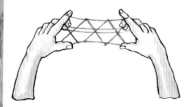

**arm** [ɑrm] 名 手臂，前肢
　　Everyone has two *arms*.
　　人人都有兩隻手臂。

**army** ['ɑrmɪ] 名　軍隊，陸軍

Dick wants to join the *army*.

迪克想從軍。

air force 空軍　navy 海軍

**around** [ə'raʊnd] 介　在……周圍，圍繞

They are running *around* the big tree.

他們正繞著大樹跑。

**arrange** [ə'rendʒ] 動　整理，分類，排列

Will you *arrange* the books on the shelf?

你把架子上的書整理一下好嗎？

**arrive** [ə'raɪv] 動　到達，到來

He will *arrive* in Taipei tomorrow morning.

明天早上他將抵達台北。

反　start 出發

注意

中國的人名、地名的拼法一般採用漢語拼音。

Taichung 台中；　Tainan 台南；　Kaohsiung 高雄；

Wang Yang 王陽；　Li Na 李娜；　Wei Pingping 魏萍萍

**arrow** ['æro] 動　箭號

Follow the *arrows* to the park.

沿著箭頭的方向就能到公園。

名　箭

My *arrow* hit the bull's eye.

我的箭射中了牛的眼睛。

**artist** ['ɑrtɪst] 名　藝術家

The young *artist* is painting.

這位年輕的藝術家正在作畫。

**A**

**as** [æz,弱 əz] 副 同樣地

He can write *as* fast *as* you can.
他能寫得和你一樣快。

連 當……時候

The bell rang *as* I was coming into the classroom.
當我正走進教室時，鈴響了。

**Asia** ['eʃə,'eʒə] 名 亞洲

We live in *Asia*.
我們居住在亞洲。

**ask** [æsk] 動 問，詢問

Mike often raises his hand to *ask*
questions in class.
在課堂上，邁克總是舉手問問題。

**asleep** [ə'slip] 形 睡著的

Sandy is *asleep* in his bed.
桑迪在床上睡著了。

反 awake 醒著的

**at** [æt,弱 ət] 介 在

Sue is not *at* the school now.
蘇現在不在學校。
She left *at* 9:00 a.m..
她是在上午9點鐘離開的。

**attention** [ə'tɛnʃən] 名 注意，留心

Pay *attention*, Tom.
湯姆，請注意。

**August** ['ɔgəst] 名 八月

The eighth month of the year was named August after a
Roman emperor.
一年的第八個月叫August，是羅馬的一位國王命名的。

**aunt** [ænt] 名 姑媽，姨媽，伯母，嬸母，舅母

Tom's *aunt* is kind to her children.
湯姆的姑媽對她的孩子們很和善。

**autumn** ['ɔtəm] 名 秋天，秋季

In the *autumn* the leaves fall from
the trees.

秋天，樹葉會從樹上落下。

**四季表示法**

spring 春季；  summer 夏季；

autumn（英）秋季；  fall（美）秋季；  winter 冬季

**awake** [ə'wek] 形 醒著的

Lucy is in bed, but she's *awake*.
露茜雖然上床了，但是她還醒著。

**away** [ə'we] 副 離，遠離

Take your dog *away* from here.
把你的狗從這裏牽走。

A

**B**

**baby** ['bebɪ] 名 嬰兒
The *baby* is sleeping.
這個嬰兒正在睡覺。

表示嬰兒性別

baby boy 男嬰； baby girl 女嬰
通常可用 it 指代嬰兒。

**back** [bæk] 名 背部，背面
A ball hit her on the *back*.
一個球打在她的後背上。

副 向後，往後
Please stand *back*.
請往後站。

**bad** [bæd] 形 壞的，惡劣的
We had *bad* weather yesterday. 昨天的天氣不好。
反 good 好的

**badge** [bædʒ] 名 徽章
There's a red *badge* on Sandy's hat.
桑迪的帽子上有一個紅徽章。

**bag** [bæg] 名 包，袋
Jim has a new *bag*.
吉姆有一個新書包。

**bake** [bek] 動 烤，烘，焙
Will you *bake* me some cookies?
請你給我烤些甜點好嗎?

**baker** ['bekɚ] 名 麵包師

　　Is he a *baker*?

　　他是一個麵包師嗎？

**balance** ['bæləns] 動 使平衡

　　Mike is *balancing* a ball on his forehead.

　　邁克正使球在額頭上保持平衡。

**B**

**balcony** ['bælkənɪ] 名 陽臺

　　The house has a *balcony*.

　　那座房子有一個陽臺。

**ball** [bɔl] 名 球，球狀物

　　Look at these *balls*.

　　看這些球。

　　球類

　　basketball 籃球;　football 足球;　baseball 棒球;　golf 高爾夫球;

　　volleyball 排球; badminton 羽毛球;　table tennis 乒乓球

**balloon** [bə'lun,bl'un] 名 氣球

　　Sue and Jane are blowing up the *balloons*.

　　蘇和珍在吹氣球。

**banana** [bə'nænə] 名 香蕉

　　Monkeys like eating *bananas*.

　　猴子喜歡吃香蕉。

**band** [bænd] 名 樂隊

　　Here comes the *band*.

　　樂隊過來了。

**bank** [bæŋk] 名 ①銀行 ②堤岸

　　①David keeps his money in the *bank*.

　　　大衛把錢存在這家銀行裏。

　　②His house is near the *bank* of the river.

　　　他的屋子靠近河岸。

**B**

**barber** ['bɑrbɚ] 名 理髮師
John is a good *barber*.
約翰是個好理髮師。

**bark** [bɑrk] 動（狗、狐等）吠叫
Tom's dog *barks* very loudly.
湯姆的狗叫得聲音很大。

**basin** ['besn̩] 名 盆,洗臉盆
Sue filled the *basin* with water.
蘇往臉盆裏接滿了水。

**basket** ['bæskɪt] 名 籃子
The *basket* is full of fruits.
這個籃子裝滿了水果。

**bat** [bæt] 名 ①球棒 ②蝙蝠
① Sandy hit the ball with a *bat*.
桑迪用球棒擊球。
② A *bat* flies at night.
蝙蝠在夜間飛行。

**bath** [bæθ] 名 洗澡
Jack is taking a *bath*.
傑克在洗澡。

**bathe** [beð] 動 洗澡，游泳
Would you like to *bathe* at home or at school?
你是願意在家還是在學校洗澡?

**bathroom** ['bæθ,rum,bæθ,rʊm] 名 洗澡間，浴室
Joan's *bathroom* is both large and bright.
瓊的浴室既寬敞又明亮。

**be** [bi,弱 bɪ] 助動 是
Will you *be* there tomorrow?
你明天到那兒去好嗎?
I'll *be* there in a minute.
我很快就會到那兒。

**beach** [bitʃ] 名 海灘，沙灘
Mike is laying on the *beach*.
邁克在海灘上躺著。

**B**

**beak** [bik] 名 鳥嘴
The bird's *beak* is red.
這隻鳥的嘴是紅色的。

**bean** [bin] 名 豆，豆類
*Beans* are good to eat.
豆子很好吃。

**bear** [bɛr,bær] 名 熊
A *bear* is a large animal with thick fur.
熊是一種長著厚厚毛皮的龐大動物。

**beard** [bɪrd] 名 鬍鬚
Santa Claus has a long white *beard*.
聖誕老人有一把長長的白鬍鬚。

**beat** [bit] 動 ①敲 ②攪拌 ③擊敗
① Jim likes *beating* a drum.
　　吉姆喜歡敲鼓。
② Diana is *beating* the eggs.
　　戴安娜正在攪勻雞蛋。
③ Mary *beat* Sue in yesterday's race.
　　瑪麗在昨天的長跑比賽中擊敗了蘇。

**beautiful** ['bjutəfəl,'bɪutəʃəl] 形 美的，美麗的
Alice has a very *beautiful* face.
艾麗斯有一張非常漂亮的臉。
反　ugly 醜的

**because** [bɪ'kɔz,bə'kɔz,bɪ'kʌz] 連 因為
I left the party *because* I felt sick.
因為覺得不舒服，我離開了晚會。

**become** [bɪ'kʌm] 動 變得，成為
I will *become* a teacher.
我將成為一名教師。

**B**

**bed** [bɛd] 名 床

**bedroom** ['bɛd,rʊm,'bɛd,rum] 名 臥室
Look at the nice bed in Sandy's bedroom.
看桑迪臥室裏這張漂亮的床。

**bee** [bi] 名 蜜蜂
I was stung by a *bee* last year.
我去年被蜜蜂螫了一下。

**beef** [bif] 名 牛肉
Billy likes *beef*. 比利喜歡吃牛肉。

**before** [bɪ'for,bɪ'fɔr] 介 在……之前
Turn off the light *before* you leave.
離開時關上燈。

**beg** [bɛg] 動 乞求，請求
The little dog *begs* for a bone.
小狗乞求得到一塊骨頭。

**begin** [bɪ'gɪn] 動 開始
School *begins* at 8:10.
學校 8 點 10 分開始上課。
同　start 開始
反　end 結束

**behind** [bɪ'haɪnd] 介 在……之後
Lucy stands *behind* Peter.
露茜站在彼得之後。
反　in front of 在……前面

**believe** [bɪ'liv] 動 相信
Helen *believed* the story.
海倫相信那個故事。
反　doubt 懷疑

## bell [bɛl] 名 鈴

Ring the *bell* at 11:30 a.m..
請在11點半打鈴。

## belong [bə'lɔŋ] 動 屬於

The book *belongs* to Jane.
這本書是珍的。

### below [bə'lo] 介 在……下面

The dog is *below* the tree.
那條狗在樹下面。

### belt [bɛlt] 名 帶，腰帶，皮帶

Dick wore a nice *belt*.
迪克繫了一條好皮帶。

## bench [bɛntʃ] 名 長凳

Jane is reading on the *bench*.
珍正坐在長凳上閱讀。

## bend [bɛnd] 動 彎曲，使彎曲

Tom is *bending* down to pick up the coin.
湯姆正彎腰去撿那枚硬幣。

## berry ['bɛrɪ] 名 漿果、草莓

A *berry* is a small juicy fruit.
草莓是一種小而多汁的水果。

## beside [bɪ'saɪd] 介 在……旁邊

There's a chair *beside* the door.
在門的旁邊有一把椅子。

### best [bɛst] 形 最好的

You are my *best* friend.
你是我最好的朋友。

反 worst 較壞的

**B**

**better** ['bɛtɚ] 形 較好的
　　I am *better* at football than you are.
　　我踢足球比你好。
　　反　worse 較壞的

**between** [bə'twin] 介 在……中間
　　Jim sits *between* Mike and Mary.
　　吉姆坐在邁克和瑪麗中間。

**bicycle** ['baɪˌsɪkḷ] 名 自行車
　　David rides a new *bicycle*.
　　大衛騎了一輛新自行車。

**big** [bɪg] 形 大的
　　Taipei is a *big* city.
　　臺北是一座大城市。
　　反　small 小的

**bill** [bɪl] 名 帳單
　　Jack paid his *bill*.
　　傑克付了他的帳。

**bird** [bɝd] 名 鳥
　　These are different kinds of *birds*.
　　這些是不同種類的鳥。

**birthday** ['bɝθˌde] 名 生日
　　Today is Lucy's *birthday*.
　　今天是露茜的生日。

**biscuit** ['bɪskɪt] 名 餅乾（英），
　　　　　　　　　　　小甜麵包（美）
　　Children like to eat *biscuits*.
　　孩子們喜歡吃餅乾。

**B**

**bite** [baɪt] 動 咬，叮

He was *bit* in his leg.
他的腿被咬了一口。

名 一口，少量

Please take a *bite* of my pizza
請嘗一嘗我的比薩餅。

注

蚊、虱、跳蚤叮咬用 bite；蜂，蝎子刺用 sting。

**bitter** ['bɪtɚ] 形 有苦味的

Black coffee has a *bitter* taste.
不加奶的咖啡有點苦味。

反 sweet 甜的

**black** [blæk] 形 黑色的

This is a *black* vase.
這是一個黑色的花瓶。

反 white 白的

**blackboard** ['blæk‚bord, 'blæk‚bɔrd] 名 黑板

Billy is drawing on the *blackboard*.
比利正在黑板上畫畫。

**blank** [blæŋk] 形 空白的，空著的

This is a piece of *blank* paper.
這是一張空白紙。

**blanket** ['blæŋkɪt] 名 毛毯，毯子

Most *blankets* are made of cotton or wool.
大部分毯子用棉花或羊毛做成。

**bleed** [blid] 動 出血，流血

Mike's nose is *bleeding*.
邁克的鼻子在流血。

**blind** [blaɪnd] 形 瞎的

Helen's grandfather is *blind*.
海倫的祖父是個盲人。

## block [blɑk] 名 積木

Lucy is playing with *blocks*.
露西在玩積木。

動 阻塞，阻擋
The fallen tree *blocked* the road.
倒地的大樹阻塞了公路。

## blood [blʌd] 名 血

Alice's *blood* type is A.
艾麗斯的血型是 A 型。

## blouse [blɑʊz,blɑʊs] 名 短外套，罩衫

Diana's *blouse* is dirty.
戴安娜的外套髒了。

## blow [blo] 動 吹

*Blow* out the candle, please.
請把蠟燭吹滅。

## blue [blu,blɪu] 形 藍色的

David's car is *blue*.
大衛的汽車是藍色的。

## board [bord,bɔrd] 動 上船（火車、飛機）

What time will we *board* the ship?
我們什麼時候上船？

名 木板
I need a bigger *board*.
我需要一塊更大的木板。

## boat [bot] 名 小船

We took a *boat* to Kinmen
我們乘船去了金門。

船的種類

boat 小船； sailing boat 帆船； motor boat 汽艇；

fishing boat 漁船； gunboat 炮艦； ship 輪船； tanker 油輪

**B**

**body** ['bɑdɪ] 名 身體，軀體

Sandy has a strong *body*.

桑迪的身體很健壯。

**boil** [bɔɪl] 動 （液體）沸騰

Did you *boil* the water?

你把水煮沸了嗎？

反 freeze 結冰

**bone** [bon] 名 骨頭

Dogs like chewing *bones*. 狗喜歡啃骨頭。

**book** [bʊk] 名 書

I love to read *books*.

我喜歡讀書。

bookmark 書籤；　bookstore（美）書店；　bookshop（英）書店；

bookseller 書商

**boot** [but] 名 靴子

His *boots* are too big.

他的靴子太大了。

**borrow** ['bɑro,'bɔro,'bɑrə] 動 借，借入

Can I *borrow* your book?

我可以借你的書嗎？

反 lend 借出

**both** [boθ] 代 兩者，雙方

I like *both* of the books.

兩本書我都喜歡。

比較

both, all 一般在句中位於 be 動詞之後，行爲動詞之前。

both 表示 "兩者都……"；all 表示 "三者或三者以上都……"。

**bother** ['bɑðɚ] 動 打擾，煩擾

Don't *bother* Peter.

不要打擾彼得。

**bottle** ['batl] 名 瓶子

These are empty *bottles*.

這些是空瓶子。

**bottom** ['batəm] 名 底，底部

A dog is at the *bottom* of the ladder.

一隻狗臥在梯子的底端。

反 top 頂部

**bounce** [bauns] 動（使）反跳，（使）彈起

Dick is *bouncing* a ball.

迪克正在拍球。

**bow** [bo] 名 ①蝴蝶結 ②弓

①Betty wears a *bow* in her hair.

貝蒂頭上繫了個蝴蝶結。

②They hunt with *bows* and arrows.

他們用弓和箭打獵。

動 鞠躬，點頭

The actor *bowed* his thanks.

那個演員鞠躬致謝。

**bowl** [bol] 名 碗

Billy holds a *bowl* of soup.

比利端著一碗湯。

**box** [baks] 名 盒子，箱子

I like the red *box*.

我喜歡那個紅盒子。

**boy** [bɔɪ] 名 男孩

Bill is a good *boy*.

比爾是個好男孩。

boyhood 少年時代

**branch** [bræntʃ] 名 樹枝

The *branch* broke off the tree.

樹枝折斷了。

**brave** [brev] 形 勇敢的
The policeman is very *brave*.
那個警察非常勇敢。

**bread** [brɛd] 名 麵包
She is cutting some *bread* for lunch.
她正在為午餐切些麵包。

**B**

**break** [brek] 動 折斷，打破
Did you *break* the dishes?
是你打破了這些碟子嗎?
反 repair 修理

**breakfast** ['brɛkfəst] 名 早飯，早餐
I have *breakfast* at 7:00 a.m..
我在早上 7 點鐘吃早點。

餐名表示法
breakfast 早餐; lunch 午餐; supper 晚餐;
tea 下午茶; dinner 正餐; meal 一頓飯

**breath** [brɛθ] 名 呼吸，氣息
Take a deep *breath*, please.
請做一下深呼吸。

**breathe** [bri ð] 動 呼吸
We *breathe* through our nose.
我們透過鼻子呼吸。

**brick** [brɪk] 名 磚
This house is made of red *bricks*.
這座房子是由紅磚砌成的。

**bridge** [brɪdʒ] 名 橋，橋梁
The *bridge* crosses a small river.
這座橋橫跨一條小河。

**bring** [brɪŋ] 動 帶來，拿來
  Peter, *bring* me a cup of tea.
  彼得，給我拿一杯茶來。
  反 take 帶走，拿走

**broom** [brum,brʊm] 名 掃帚
  Diana sweeps the floor with a *broom*.
  戴安娜用掃帚掃地。

**brother** ['brʌðə] 名 兄弟
  Billy has one *brother*.
  比利有一個兄弟。

**brown** [braʊn] 形 棕色的，咖啡色的，褐色的
  David likes *brown* clothes.
  大衛喜歡棕色服裝。

**brush** [brʌʃ] 名 刷子，毛刷
  I lost my hair *brush*.
  我的梳子丟了。
  Chinese brush 毛筆

  動 刷，擦
  Tom is *brushing* his teeth.
  湯姆正在刷牙。

**bubble** ['bʌbl̩] 名 氣泡
  Ella is blowing soap *bubbles*.
  埃拉在吹肥皂泡。

**build** [bɪld] 動 建築，造
  The girls are *building* a house
  with blocks.
  女孩們在用積木搭房子。

**building** ['bɪldɪŋ] 名 建築物
  Look at all the *buildings*.
  看這些建築物。

**bump** [bʌmp] 名 腫塊

There is a *bump* on my leg.
我的腿上有個包。

動 碰，撞

I *bumped* into Lisa yesterday.
昨天我偶然遇到了莉莎。

**B**

**bunch** [bʌntʃ] 名 串，束

Mike brings a *bunch* of flowers to Jane.
邁克給珍帶來一束花。

**burn** [bɜn] 動 燃燒

I *burnt* dinner last night.
昨晚我把飯燒焦了。

**burst** [bɜst] 動 爆炸，炸裂

Jane's balloon *burst*.
珍的氣球爆炸了。

**bury** ['bɛrɪ] 動 埋葬

The boys *buried* the dead bird.
男孩們埋葬了那隻死鳥。

**bus** [bʌs] 名 公共汽車

**bus stop** 公共汽車站

People wait for a bus at the *bus stop*.
人們在公共汽車站等公共汽車。

**busy** ['bɪzɪ] 形 忙的，繁忙的

Rose is *busy* with her homework.
羅斯正忙著做家庭作業。

反 free 有空的

**but** [bʌt] 連 但是

Sandy likes ice cream *but* he doesn't like peas.
桑迪喜歡冰淇淋，但是他不喜歡豌豆。

**butcher** ['butʃɚ] 名 屠夫，賣肉者

His mother often buys meat from the *butcher*.

他媽媽通常從那個肉商那裏買肉。

**butter** ['bʌtɚ] 名 奶油

Put some *butter* on the bread, please.

請往麵包上塗些奶油。

**butterfly** ['bʌtɚ,flaɪ] 名 蝴蝶

Most *butterflies* are beautiful.

大多數的蝴蝶都很美麗。

**button** ['bʌtn] 名 鈕扣，按鈕

Push the *button*, please.

請按一下按鈕。

**buy** [baɪ] 動 動，買

I *bought* a new dress.

我買了一條新裙子。

反 sell 賣

**by** [baɪ] 介 ①在……旁邊 ②到……爲止
③靠，用

① Sandy and her sister are standing

*by* the bus stop and waiting for the bus.

桑迪和姐姐站在公共汽車站旁等車。

② Her mother will come back *by* 1:00 at noon.

中午，她媽媽最遲1點回來。

③ She goes to work *by* car.

她開車上班。

注

by 表示 "用某種手段，方法"，with 表示
"用某種工具"。

**cage** [kedʒ] 名 籠子

There are two birds in this *cage*.

這只籠子裏有兩隻鳥。

**cake** [kek] 名 蛋糕

A *cake* is made from flour,
eggs, butter and sugar.

蛋糕是由麵粉、雞蛋、奶油和糖做成的。

**calendar** [ˈkæləndɚˌˈkælɪndɚ] 名 日曆

There's a *calendar* on the desk.

桌子上有一本日曆。

**call** [kɔl] 動 ①打電話 ②叫，呼喚 ③叫做，稱呼

① Someone is *calling* me.

　有人正在給我打電話。

② Please *call* me at six o'clock.

　請在6點鐘叫醒我。

③ Kate *calls* her cat Mimi.

　凱特把她的貓叫做咪咪。

call box 公用電話亭

**camera** [ˈkæmərə] 名 照相機

Alice's *camera* is new.

艾麗斯的照相機是新的。

camp

## camp [kæmp] 動 宿營，露營
Let's go *camping*.
咱們去露營吧。

## can [kæn, 弱 kən] 名 罐頭，一（罐）
Diana opened a *can* of meat.
戴安娜打開了一罐肉罐頭。

助動 能
Jim *can* swim.
吉姆會游泳。

## Canada ['kænədə] 名 加拿大
*Canada* is a country in North America.
加拿大是北美洲的一個國家。

## candle ['kændl] 名 蠟燭
Just one *candle* is on the big cake.
大蛋糕上只有一支蠟燭。

## candy ['kændɪ] 名 糖果
The children often buy *candy* from this store.
孩子們經常在這個商店裏買糖果。

## cap [kæp] 名 帽子
Whose *cap* is this?
這是誰的帽子？

## capital ['kæpətl] 名 首都
Beijing is the *capital* of China.
北京是中國的首都。

## car [kɑr] 名 小汽車
What a nice *car!*
多漂亮的小汽車啊！

## card [kɑrd] 名 卡片
Helen sent Betty a birthday *card*.
海倫寄給貝蒂一張生日賀卡。

**care** [kɛr,kær] 動 關心，照顧
Kate *cares* for her kitten.
凱特照顧她的小貓。

名 關心，照顧
Take *care* of yourself!
請多保重。

**careful** ['kɛrfəl,'kærfəl] 形 小心的，仔細的
Be *careful*!
小心點!
反 careless 粗心的

**careless** ['kɛrlɪs,'kærlɪs] 形 粗心的，馬虎的
Dick is *careless* when he does his homework.
迪克做作業時很粗心。

**carpet** ['kɑrpɪt] 名 地毯，毛毯
A cat is lying on the *carpet*.
一隻貓正躺在地毯上。

**carrot** ['kærət] 名 胡蘿蔔
John's father bought many *carrots*.
約翰的父親買了許多胡蘿蔔。

**carry** ['kærɪ] 動 攜帶，搬運
Will you *carry* the plate of cakes?
你端著這盤蛋糕好嗎?

**cartoon** [kɑr'tun] 名 卡通，動畫片
The *cartoons* on TV made Dick laugh.
電視上的卡通逗得吉姆大笑。

**carve** [kɑrv] 動 刻，雕刻，刻字
Peter *carved* his name on the stone.
彼得把他的名字刻在石頭上。

**case** [kes] 名 箱子，盒子
Jack is carrying a *case* of coke.
傑克正在搬運一箱可樂。

## cat [kæt] 名 貓
The *cat* likes fish.
貓喜歡吃魚。

## catch [kætʃ] 動 抓住，接住
Mary *catches* the ball.
瑪麗接住了球。
反 miss 錯過

## catch up 趕上
The snail can't *catch up* with the rabbit.
蝸牛趕不上兔子。

## cave [kev] 名 洞穴
Don't go into the *cave*.
不要進這個山洞。

## ceiling ['silɪŋ] 名 天花板
Jack is painting the *ceiling*.
傑克正在給天花板刷油漆。

## celebrate ['sɛlə,bret] 動 慶祝
The children are *celebrating* Billy's birthday.
孩子們正在慶祝比利的生日。

## cent [sɛnt] 名 分(貨幣單位)
One hundred *cents* is one dollar.
一百美分是一美元。

## center ['sɛntɚ] 名 (美)
## centre ['sɛntɚ] 名 (英) 中心，中央
Helen is standing in the *centre* of the circle.
海倫正站在圓的中心。

## certainly ['sɚtənlɪ,'sɚtnlɪ,'sɚtɪnlɪ] 副 (口) 當然，當然可以
"May I have a look?" "*Certainly*."
"我可以看一看嗎？" "當然可以。"

**chair** [tʃɛr,tʃær] 名 椅子
Is your *chair* brown?
你的椅子是棕色的嗎?

**chalk** [tʃɔk] 名 粉筆
Peter likes drawing with *chalk*.
彼得喜歡用粉筆畫畫。

**chance** [tʃæns] 名 機會
Give me another *chance*.
再給我一次機會吧。

**change** [tʃendʒ] 動 變換,改變
Please *change* your mind.
請你換個想法。
*Change* your shirt.
換換你的襯衫。

**chase** [tʃes] 動 追趕,追逐
The dog *chased* the cat, but the
cat climbed the tree.
狗去追趕那隻貓,但是貓爬上了樹。

**chat** [tʃæt] 名 閒談,聊天
Let's have a *chat*.
讓我們閒談一會。

**cheap** [tʃip] 形 便宜的
Tomatoes are *cheap* at the moment.
目前,蕃茄便宜。
反 expensive 昂貴的

**check** [tʃɛk] 動 檢查
*Check* your homework after you
finish it.
你做完作業後檢查一下。
名 (餐館) 帳單
Can we have the *check*, please?
我可以看一下帳單嗎?

C

**cheek** [tʃik] 名 面頰，臉蛋
Lucy is pointing at her *cheeks*.
露茜正指著她的面頰。

**cheer** [tʃɪr] 名 歡呼，喝采
Three *cheers* for Billy.
為比利叫歡呼三次。

動 歡呼，喝采
Let's *cheer*!
讓我們歡呼吧!

**cheese** [tʃiz] 名 起士，乳酪
*Cheese* is a kind of food made from milk.
起士是一種由牛奶製成的食品。

**chemist** [ˈkɛmɪst] 名 化學家
Dick's uncle is a *chemist*.
迪克的叔叔是一位化學家。

**chess** [tʃɛs] 名 西洋棋
Alice's father plays *chess* well.
艾麗斯的父親西洋棋下得很好。

**chew** [tʃu,tʃɪu] 動 咀嚼，嚼碎
We *chew* with our teeth.
我們用牙齒咀嚼食物。
chewing gum　口香糖

**chicken** [ˈtʃɪkɪn,ˈtʃɪkən] 名 小雞，雞肉
Here are four *chickens*.
這兒有四隻小雞。

**child** [tʃaɪld] 名 小孩
The *child* is laughing.
那個小孩正在笑。
childhood　幼年時代，童年

**children** ['tʃɪldrən] 名 孩子們

The *children* went into the classroom.

孩子們走進了教室。

**chimney** ['tʃɪmnɪ] 名 煙囪

There is a nest in their *chimney*.

他們的煙囪裡有個鳥窩。

**China** ['tʃaɪnə] 名 中國

Shanghai is in the east of *China*.

上海在中國的東部。

**chocolate** ['tʃɑkəlɪt,'tʃɔkəlɪt] 名 巧克力

Billy loves *chocolate*.

比利愛吃巧克力。

**C**

**choose** [tʃuz]↔ 動 選擇，挑選

*Choose* the best one.

選擇最好的一個。

**chop** [tʃɑp] 動 砍，劈

Mike is *chopping* the wood.

邁克正在劈木頭。

**chopsticks** ['tʃɔp,stɪks] 名 筷子

Tom is trying to hold the ball with a pair of *chopsticks*.

湯姆正試著用一雙筷子來球。

**Christmas** ['krɪsməs] 名 聖誕節

Merry *Christmas!* 聖誕節快樂!

西方國家主要節日

Christmas Day 聖誕節（12 月 25 日）;

Thanksgiving 感恩節（11 月的第四個星期日）;

Father's Day 父親節（8 月 8 日）;

Mother's Day 母親節（5 月的第二個星期日）;

April Fool's Day 愚人節（4 月 1 日）;

Easter 復活節（每節春分月圓後第一個星期日）

## church [tʃɜtʃ] 名 教堂

My grandmother goes to *church* every Sunday.
我奶奶每個星期天都去教堂。

## cinema ['sɪnəmə] 名 電影院

Let's go to the *cinema*.
我們去看電影吧。

## circle ['sɜkl] 名 圓圈

Draw small *circles*. 畫些小圓圈。

## circus ['sɜkəs] 名 馬戲團，雜技場

I had a good time at the *circus* yesterday.
昨天我看馬戲團看得很開心。

## city ['sɪtɪ] 名 城市

There are many buildings and cars in a *city*.
城市裏有許多高樓和汽車。

## clap [klæp] 動 鼓掌，拍手

People began to *clap* and cheer.
人們開始鼓掌歡呼。

## class [klæs] 名 ①班級 ②課

① There are forty pupils in this *class*.
這個班裏有 40 名學生。
② We have no *classes* on Saturday.
我們星期六不上課。

## classroom ['klæs,rum,'klæs,rʊm] 名 教室

This is our new *classroom*.
這是我們的新教室。

## claw [klɔ] 名 爪子

The cat has sharp *claws*.
貓有尖利的爪子。

## clean [klin] 形 清潔的，乾淨的

Her room is *clean*. 她的房間很乾淨。
反 dirty 髒的

**clear** [klɪr] 形 清澈的，晴朗的
The day is *clear* today.
今天天氣晴朗。

**clerk** [klɜk] 名 職員，辦事員
Mary's aunt is a bank *clerk*.
瑪麗的姑姑是一個銀行職員。

**clever** [klɛvɚ] 形 聰明的，伶俐的
Rose is a *clever* girl.
羅絲是個聰明的女孩。
反 stupid 笨拙的

**climb** [klaɪm] 動 爬，攀登
They'll *climb* the Great Wall this Sunday.
這個星期天他們將去爬長城。

**clock** [klɑk] 名 時鐘
My *clock* is fast.
我的時鐘快了。

**close** [kloz] 動 關，閉
Will you *close* the door, please?
請關上門好嗎？
反 open 打開

**closed** [klozd] 形 關閉的
The shop is *closed*.
那個商店不開門。
反 open 開著的

**clothes** [kloz,kloðz] 名 衣服
Betty has a lot of *clothes*.
貝蒂有許多衣服。

clothing 衣服總稱; dress 女服，連衣裙;

suit 西裝; coat 上衣; overcoat 大衣;

shirt 男襯衫; jacket 夾克; blouse 女襯衣,罩衫;

raincoat 雨衣; uniform 制服; robe 長袍

## cloud [klaʊd] 名 雲

There are white *clouds* in the sky.
藍天上飄著朵朵白雲。

## clown [klaʊn] 名 小丑

*Clowns* always wear funny clothes.
小丑們總穿著滑稽衣服。

## coach [kotʃ] 名 教練員

Who is the *coach* of the football team?
誰是這支足球隊的教練員?

## coast [kost] 名 海濱

The Whites spent their holidays by the *coast*.
懷特一家在海濱度過了假期。

### cock [kɑk] 名 公鷄

The *cock* crows at dawn. 公鷄報曉。

### coffee ['kɔfɪ] 名 咖啡

Diana drinks *coffee* for breakfast.
戴安娜早餐時喝咖啡。

## coin [kɔɪn] 名 硬幣

Jim collected many *coins*.
吉姆搜集了許多硬幣。

## cold [kold] 形 寒冷的

It's very *cold*. 天氣非常冷。
反 hot 熱的

名 感冒
I have a *cold*. 我感冒了。

### collect [kə'lɛkt] 動 搜集

Rose *collects* stamps as a hobby.
羅絲愛好集郵。

**college** [ˈkɑlɪdʒ] 名 大學，學院

Helen wants to study at a *college*.

海倫想去大學學習。

注

通常綜合性大學用 university 表示，學院用 college 表示。

**colour** [ˈkʌlɚ] 名（英）

**color** [ˈkʌlɚ] 名（美）　　顏色

What *color* do you like best?

你最喜歡什麼顏色？

**comb** [kom] 名 梳子

Kate has a blue *comb*.

凱特有一把藍梳子。

動 梳理

Now she's *combing* her hair.

現在她正在梳理頭髮。

**come** [kʌm] 動 來

*Come* here. 過來。

反 go 去

**compare** [kəmˈpɛr] 動 比較

They're *comparing* their each shoes.

他們正在比較他們各自的鞋。

**computer** [kəmˈpjutɚ, kəmˈpɪutɚ]

名 電腦

Alice can use a *computer*.

艾麗斯會使用電腦。

**concert** [ˈkɑnsɝt] 名 音樂會

They will give a *concert* next week.

他們在下周將舉行一場音樂會。

**confuse** [kənˈfjuz, kənˈfɪuz] 動 混淆；使混亂

The driver is *confused* by the signs.

這個司機被那些路標弄糊塗了。

黄衣服
yellow clothes

灰色的驢
gray donkey

橘紅色氣球
orange balloon

綠褲子
green trousers

深藍色沙發
dark blue sofa

紫連衣裙
purple dress

黑色車
black car

紅色夾克
red jacket

藍外套
blue coat

棕色的琴
brown cello

粉紅的圍巾
pink scarf

白鬍子
white beard

## connect [kə'nɛkt] 動 連接，連結
The two cities are *connected* by a highway.
這兩個城市被一條高速公路連接起來。
反 divide 分開

## control [kən'trol] 名 控制器
動 控制
Billy *controls* the robot by remote control.
比利通過搖控器控制機器人。

## cook [kʊk] 名 廚師
Jack is a *cook*, too.
傑克也是一名廚師。

動 烹調，煮
I will *cook* dinner tomorrow.
明天我做晚飯。

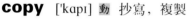

## cool [kul] 形 涼爽，涼的
It's *cool* this evening.
今天晚上很涼快。
反 warm 暖和的

## copy ['kɑpɪ] 動 抄寫，複製
*Copy* the words on the blackboard, please.
請抄寫黑板上的單字。

## corn [kɔrn] 名 玉米（美），小麥（英）
We like boiled *corn*.
我們喜歡吃煮熟的玉米。

## corner ['kɔrnɚ] 名 角，角落
There is a big tree at the *corner* of the street.
街道的拐角處有一顆大樹。

## cost [kɔst] 動 價值爲，花費
The book *costs* 50 dollars.
這本書價格爲五十元。

**cotton** ['kɑtn̩] 名 棉花

This shirt is made of *cotton*.

這件襯衣是全棉的。

**cough** [kɔf] 名 咳嗽

Sue has a bad *cough*.

蘇咳嗽得很屬害。

**C**

**count** [kaʊnt] 動 數，點

*Count* from one to ten, please.

請從 1 數到 10。

**country** ['kʌntrɪ] 名 ①國家 ②鄉下

① There are many *countries* in the world.

世界上有很多國家。

② His parents live in the *country*.

他的父母住在鄉下。

**cousin** ['kʌzn̩] 名 表（堂）兄弟，
表（堂）姐妹

How many *cousins* do you have?

你有幾個表兄妹?

**cover** ['kʌvɚ] 動 遮，蓋

*Cover* your eyes!

閉上你的眼睛!

**cow** [kaʊ] 名 母牛，乳牛

*Cows* give us milk.

乳牛向我們提供牛奶。

**cowboy** ['kaʊ,bɔɪ] 名 牛仔，牧童

The *cowboy* looks after the cows.

那個牧童照顧那些乳牛。

**crab** [kræb] 名 蟹

We catch *crabs* at the seaside.

我們在海邊捉螃蟹。

## crawl [krɔl] 動 爬

A baby *crawls* before he(she) can walk.
嬰兒會走路前先學會爬。

## crayon ['kreən] 名 蠟筆

Mary has twelve *crayons*.
瑪麗有12支蠟筆。

### cream [krim] 名 奶油，乳脂

I like my coffee with *cream* and sugar.
我喜歡喝加牛奶和糖的咖啡。

### create [krɪ'et] 動 創造

The man *created* a robot.
那個人造出了一個機器人。

## crocodile ['krɑkəˌdaɪl] 名 鱷魚

A *crocodile* lives in hot areas of the world.
鱷魚生活在世界上的熱帶地區。

## cross [krɔs] 名 十字（架）

There is a red *cross* on the box.
盒子上印有一個紅色的十字。

動 穿越
*Cross* the street carefully.
過馬路要小心。

## crouch [kraʊtʃ] 動 蹲

Dick *crouches* behind the sofa.
迪克蹲在沙發後面。

### crow [kro] 名 烏鴉

The sound of the *crow* is harsh.
烏鴉的叫聲刺耳。

### crowd [kraʊd] 名 人群

There were a big *crowd* at the football ground yesterday.
昨天足球場上擠滿了人群。

**crown** [kraʊn] 名 王冠

The king wears a beautiful *crown*.

國王戴著一頂漂亮的王冠。

**crush** [krʌʃ] 動 壓碎、壓扁

I *crushed* the soda can.

我壓扁了汽水罐。

**C**

**cry** [kraɪ] 動 哭

Why is the baby *crying*?

為什麼這個嬰兒一直在哭？

比較

cry 放聲大哭，weep 低聲啜泣

**cup** [kʌp] 名 茶杯

Diana is pouring some tea into the *cups*.

戴安娜正在往那些茶杯裏倒茶。

**cupboard** ['kʌbəd] 名 碗櫃

We put bowls and plates in the *cupboard*.

我們把碗和盤子都放在碗櫃裏。

**curry** ['kɜɪ] 名 咖哩

I like the taste of *curry*.

我愛吃咖哩菜。

**cushion** ['kʊʃən,'kʊʃɪn] 名 坐墊，椅墊

Jane sits on a blue *cushion*.

珍坐在一個藍椅墊上。

**curtain** ['kɜtn] 名 窗簾

Please close the *curtains*.

請拉上窗簾。

**cut** [kʌt] 動 切、割、剪

Sue can *cut* paper dolls.

蘇會剪紙娃娃。

**cute** [kjut,kıut] 形 令人喜愛的，漂亮的
　　　Isn't she a *cute* baby?
　　　難道她不是一個漂亮的嬰兒嗎？

**cycle** ['saɪkḷ] 名 腳踏車
　　　He bought a new *cycle* yesterday.
　　　他昨天買了一輛新腳踏車。

**dad** [dæd] 名 爸爸
Good morning, *dad*.
早安，爸爸。

**daily** ['delɪ] 形 日常的，每日的
This is a *daily* newspaper.
這是一份日報。
daily life 日常生活
China Daily 中國時報

**dance** [dæns] 名 舞會
They'll go to the *dance* tonight.
今晚他們要去參加舞會。
動 跳舞
Mary *dances* very well.
瑪麗跳舞跳得很好。

**dancer** ['dænsɚ] 名 舞蹈家
She wants to be a *dancer*.
她想成為一名舞蹈家。

**danger** ['dendʒɚ] 名 危險
Dick, do you see the *danger* sign?
迪克,你看見危險標誌了嗎?

## dangerous ['den(ə)rəs] 形 危險的

It's *dangerous* to go into the cave.
進入那個洞穴是危險的。
反 safe 安全的

**D**

## dare [dɛr,dær] 動 敢

Jack doesn't *dare* to touch the snake.
傑克不敢摸蛇。

## dark [dɑrk] 形 黑暗的

It's *dark* in the cave.
山洞裏很暗。
反 bright 明亮的

### dash [dæʃ] 動 猛衝，急奔

A dog is *dashing* across the road.
一條狗正穿過馬路。

### date [det] 名 日期

"What's the *date* today?" "It's May 6."
"今天是幾月幾號?" "今天是5月6日。"

## daughter ['dɔtɚ] 名 女兒

Mr. White has a *daughter* and a son.
懷特先生有一個女兒和一個兒子。

## day [de] 名 天，白天

There are seven *days* in a week.
一個星期有7天。

時間表示法

second 秒; minute 分; quarter 一刻鐘; hour 小時; day 天;
week 星期; month 月; year 年; century 世紀

## dead [dɛd] 形 死的

The bird is *dead*.
這隻鳥死了。
反 alive 活著的

**deaf** [dɛf] 形 聾的

Helen Keller was *deaf*.

海倫·凱勒耳朵聾了。

**D**

**dear** [dɪr] 形 ①親愛的 ②昂貴的

① You are my *dear* friend.

　你是我的好朋友。

② The car is *dear* to me.

　對我來說,這輛小汽車非常昂貴。

**December** [di'sɛmbɚ] 名 十二月

*December* is the last month of the year.

十二月是一年裏最後一個月。

**decide** [dɪ'saɪd] 動 決定

Mary can't *decide* what to do.

瑪麗無法決定做什麼好。

**decorate** ['dɛkə,ret] 動 裝飾

Alice is *decorating* the room for our party.

艾麗斯正在為我們的晚會裝飾房間。

**deep** [dip] 形 深的

The sea is very *deep*.

大海是非常深的。

反 shallow 淺的

**delicious** [dɪ'lɪʃəs] 形 味道好的

This apple is *delicious*.

這個蘋果真好吃。

**deliver** [dɪ'lɪvɚ] 動 傳遞, 投遞

A mailman *delivers* parcels and letters.

投遞員投遞包裹和信件。

**dentist** ['dɛntɪst] 名 牙科醫生

The *dentist* is examining Sandy's teeth.

那個牙醫正在查看桑迪的牙齒。

## desert  ['dɛzɚt] 名 沙漠
There is little water in the *desert*.
沙漠裏水十分稀少。

## desk  [dɛsk] 名 課桌
Rose is reading at her *desk*.
羅絲正在書桌前讀書。

## dessert  [dɪ'zɝt] 名 甜點
Sandy wants an ice cream for *dessert*.
桑迪想要一支冰淇淋作爲甜點。

## destroy  [dɪ'strɔɪ] 動 破壞，摧壞
The fire *destroyed* the whole factory.
火災燒毀了整個工廠。

## dial  ['daɪ(ə)l] 動 撥電話
Mary *dialed* the wrong number.
瑪麗撥錯了電話號碼。

## diamond  ['daɪ(ə)mənd] 名 鑽石
A *diamond* costs a lot of money.
一顆鑽石值好多錢。

## diary  ['daɪərɪ] 名 日記
Helen keeps a *diary* every day.
海倫每天堅持寫日記。

## dictionary  ['dɪkʃən͵ɛrɪ] 名 字典，辭典
Jane has an English pocket *dictionary*.
珍有一本英語袖珍辭典。

## die  [daɪ] 動 死
The deer *died* of old age.
那隻鹿老死了。
名 骰子
Please roll the *die*.
請你擲骰子。

**D**

**difference** ['dɪf(ə)rəns] 名 不同之處
Point out the *differences* between China and America.
指出中美兩國的不同。

**different** ['dɪf(ə)rənt] 形 不同的
Blue and green are *different* colors.
藍色和綠色是不同的顏色。
反 same 相同的

**difficult** ['dɪfəˌkʌlt] 形 困難的，難的
This text is too *difficult*.
這篇文章太難了。
反 easy 容易的

**dig** [dɪg] 動 挖
The two mice are *digging* the hole.
這兩隻老鼠正在挖洞。

**dining room** [ˈdaɪnɪŋ ˌrum] 名 餐廳
We eat our meals in the *dining room*.
我們在餐室吃飯。

**dinner** ['dɪnɚ] 名 一日裏的正餐，晚餐
Have you had *dinner* yet?
你吃過晚飯了嗎？

**dinosaur** ['daɪnəˌsɔr] 名 恐龍
Now you can't see real *dinosaurs*.
現在你看不見真恐龍了。

**direct** [dəˈrɛkt,daɪˈrɛkt] 動 指導，指揮
The policeman is *directing* the traffic.
這個警察正在指揮交通。

**dirty** ['dɝtɪ] 形 髒的
Dick, wash your *dirty* hands first.
迪克，先去洗洗你的髒手。

## disappear [ˌdɪsə'pɪr] 動 消失
The sun *disappeared* behind clouds.
太陽消失在雲朵後面。

## discover [dɪs'kʌvɚ] 動 發現
Columbus *discovered* America.
哥倫布發現了美洲。

## discuss [dɪ'skʌs] 動 討論，談論
They are *discussing* the question.
他們正在討論這個問題。

## dish [dɪʃ] 名 盤子，碟子
Diana is washing the *dishes*.
戴安娜正在洗碟子。

## display [dɪ'sple] 動 展示，陳列
The new books are *displayed* in the window.
那些新書陳列在櫥窗裏。

## disturb [dɪ'stɝb] 動 打擾，擾亂
Do not *disturb*.
請勿打擾。

## dive [daɪv] 動 跳水
I will *dive* into the swimming pool.
我要跳進游泳池裏。

## divide [də'vaɪd] 動 劃分，分開
Betty *divides* the cake into four parts.
貝蒂把蛋糕分成 4 份。

## do [du,弱 dʊ,də] 動 做，幹
Billy is *doing* his homework.
比利正在做作業。

用於構成疑問句、否定句時, do 本身無詞義。
"*Do* you like bananas?" "Yes, I *do*."
"你喜歡吃香蕉嗎?" "是的，我喜歡。"

I prefer *pineapple* to bananas.
我喜歡吃鳳梨，而不喜歡吃香蕉。

do 的用法

| 人稱 | 單數 | 複數 |
|---|---|---|
| 1 | I do | We do |
| 2 | You do | You do |
| 3 | He (She, It) does | They do |

**D**

## doctor ['dɑktɚ] 名 醫生
Mike needs to see the *doctor*.
邁克需要去看病。

### dog [dɔg] 名 狗
Tom likes *dog*s.
湯姆喜歡狗。

### doll [dɑl,dɔl] 名 玩具娃娃
Lucy has three *doll*s.
露茜有三個布娃娃。

## dollar ['dɑlɚ] 名 美元，元
Sandy gave one *dollar* to Sue.
桑迪給了蘇一美元。

## donkey ['dɑŋkɪ,'dɔŋkɪ] 名 驢
A *donkey* can carry heavy things for people.
驢能幫助人們運送重物。

## door [dor,dɔr] 名 門
Open the *door*, please.
請開門。

## dot [dɑt] 名 點
There are five *dots* on this paper.
這張紙上有5個點。

**double** ['dʌbḷ] 形 雙倍的，成雙的

There's a *double* bed in the room.

房間裏有一張雙人床。

**down** [daʊn] 副 向下

Sit *down*, please.

請坐下。

反 up 向上

**downstairs** ['daʊn'stɛrz,daʊn'stærz] 副 往樓下

Sue is going *downstairs* for breakfast.

蘇正下樓去吃早點。

**dozen** ['dʌzṇ] 名 十二個，一打

Her mother bought a *dozen* of eggs.

她媽媽買了一打鷄蛋。

**dragon** ['drægən] 名 龍

I read some stories about *dragons*.

我讀了一些關於龍的故事。

**dragonfly** ['drægən,flaɪ] 名 蜻蜓

A *dragonfly* is a good insect.

蜻蜓是益蟲。

**draw** [drɔ] 名 畫

Billy is *drawing* a picture.

比利正在畫一張畫。

**drawer** [drɔr] 名 抽屜

Peter put the keys into the *drawer*.

彼得把鑰匙放進那個抽屜。

**dream** [drim] 名 做夢

Alice had a good *dream*.

艾麗斯做了一個好夢。

動 夢(想)

She *dreamed* that she was flying.

她夢見自己在飛。

**D**

**dress** [drɛs] 名 ① 女服（統稱） ② 連衣裙

① Those are pretty *dresses*.
多麼漂亮的女服啊！

② Betty wears a yellow *dress*.
貝蒂穿著一件黃色連衣裙。

**drink** [drɪŋk] 動 喝

I *drink* coffee in the morning.
我在早晨喝咖啡。

名 飲料

Do you want a *drink*?
你想來杯飲料嗎?

**drip** [drɪp] 動 滴落，滴下

The rain *drips* from the ceiling.
雨水從天花板上滴下來。

**drive** [draɪv] 動 駕駛

Can you *drive*?
你會開車嗎?

**driver** ['draɪvɚ] 名 司機

Tom's uncle is a taxi *driver*.
湯姆的叔叔是一個計程車司機。

**drop** [drɑp] 動 落下，掉下

He *dropped* the teapot on the floor.
他把茶壺掉在地上了。

**drum** [drʌm] 名 鼓

What a big *drum*!
多麼大的一個鼓啊！

**dry** [draɪ] 形 乾的

The clothes are *dry*.
這些衣服是乾的。

反 wet 濕的

**D**

## duck [dʌk] 名 鴨子(雌)

A *duck* can walk and swim.
鴨子既能在地上行走，也會在水中游泳。

## duckling ['dʌklɪŋ] 名 小鴨，幼鴨

Do you like this *duckling*?
你喜歡這隻小鴨嗎？

## dumb [dʌm] 形 啞的

That pupil is *dumb*.
那個學生是個啞巴。

## during ['dɪʊrɪŋ,'djʊrɪŋ] 介 在……期間

*During* summer vacation, David went to England.
暑假期間大衛去了英國。

## dust [dʌst] 名 塵土

The room is covered with *dust*.
房間布滿了灰塵。

## dustbin ['dʌst,bɪn] 名 垃圾箱

## duster ['dʌstɚ] 名 抹布，撢子

Jack cleans the table with a *duster*.
傑克用抹布擦桌子。

## duty ['djutɪ,'d(ɪ)utɪ] 名 任務

Who's on *duty* today?
今天誰值日？

**each** [itʃ] 形 各自（的），每
*Each* child has a hat.
每個孩子都有一頂帽子。
代 每個，各自
*Each* of us has an English notebook.
我們每人都有一個英語筆記本。

**eagle** [ˈigḷ] 名 鷹
The *eagle* is flying above our heads.
鷹在我們頭頂上飛。

**ear** [ɪr] 名 耳朵
A rabbit has two long *ears*.
兔子有兩隻大耳朵。

**early** [ˈɝlɪ] 副 早
We should go to bed *early*.
我們應該早早上床睡覺。
形 早的
It's *early*, they aren't up.
天還早，他們還沒起床。
反 late 遲的

**earn** [ɝn] 動 賺得
He wants to *earn* a lot of money.
他想賺好多錢。
反 spend 花費

## earth [ɜθ] 名 ①地球 ②泥土

① The *earth* moves around the sun.
地球繞著太陽轉。

**天體**

sun 太陽; earth 地球; moon 月亮; star 星星；

planet 行星; satellite 衛星; comet 慧星

② Carrots grow in the *earth*.
胡蘿蔔在土裏生長。

## earthquake [ɜθ'kwek] 名 地震

Some houses were destroyed in the *earthquake*.
一些房屋在地震中被毀。

## east [ist] 名 東方

The sun rises in the *east*.
太陽從東方升起。

形 東方的，東部的
The *east* wind is blowing.
現在刮東風。

反 west 西方，西方的; south 南方，南方的; north 北方，北方的

## easy ['izɪ] 形 容易的

The test was *easy*.
這次考試很容易。

## eat [it] 動 吃

Kate often *eats* some biscuits for lunch.
凱特經常在午餐時吃些餅乾。

## egg [ɛg] 名 鷄蛋

The *egg* is broken.
鷄蛋破了。

## eight [et] 數 八

There are *eight* books on the shelf.
書架上有 8 本書。

**E**

**eighteen**  [e'tin,'e'tin] 數 十八

Nine and nine makes *eighteen*.

9 加 9 等於 18

**eighty**  ['etɪ] 數 八十

Turn to Page *Eighty*.

翻到第 80 頁。

**either**  ['iðɚ,'aɪðɚ] 形（兩者之中）任一的

You may use *either* pen.

你可用這兩枝筆中的任何一枝。

連 或者，要麼（用於表達兩者之中，任選一個）

Put it *either* on the table or in the drawer.

把它放在桌子上，或者放進抽屜裏。

*Either* be quiet or leave.

請安靜，不然就出去。

**elbow**  ['ɛlˌbo] 名 肘

Don't put your *elbows* on the table.

不要把手肘放在桌子上。

**electricity**  [ɪˌlɛk'trɪsətɪ,ɪlɛk'trɪsətɪ] 名 電

You are wasting *electricity*.

你在浪費電。

**elephant**  ['ɛləfənt] 名 大象

*Elephant* is the largest animal
on land.

大象是陸地上最大的動物。

**eleven**  [ɪ'lɛvən] 數 十一

There are *eleven* apples in the basket.

籃子裏有 11 個蘋果。

**else**  [ɛls] 形 別的

Do you want anything *else*?

你還想要些別的東西嗎?

## employ [ɪm'plɔɪ] 動 雇用

We *employ* an office cleaner.
我們雇用了一位辦公室清潔工。

## empty ['ɛmptɪ] 形 空的

The box is *empty*.
那個盒子是空的。
反 full 滿的

## end [ɛnd] 名 末端，盡頭

Our school is at the *end* of the street.
我們學校在街道的盡頭。

動 結束
The party *ended*.
晚會結束了。

### enemy ['ɛnəmɪ] 名 敵人

He is not my *enemy*.
他不是我的敵人。
反 friend 朋友

### engine ['ɛndʒən] 名 發動機

If the *engine* doesn't work, the car can't go.
如果發動機壞了，汽車就不能行駛了。

## England ['ɪŋglənd]· 名 英國

*England* is an island country.
英國是一個島國。

注
England 廣義指"英國"，實際上 England（英格蘭）與 Scotland，Wales（威爾士）一樣，是英倫三島的一部分。

英國全稱

the United Kingdom of Great Britain and Northern Ireland 簡寫爲UK。

**English** [ˈɪŋglɪʃ] 名 英語

Do you speak *English*?

你講英語嗎?

形 英國的

This is an *English* soldier.

這是一名英國士兵。

**enjoy** [ɪnˈdʒɔɪ] 動 喜愛,享受……樂趣

She *enjoys* watching TV plays.

她喜歡看電視劇。

**enough** [ɪˈnʌf,əˈnʌf] 形 足够的

That's *enough*.

那足够了。

**enter** [ˈɛntɚ] 動 進,入

The dog *entered* the room.

那條狗進入房間。

**entrance** [ˈɛntrəns] 名 入口,門口

Mr. White came to the *entrance* of the building.

懷特先生來到了大樓的入口處。

**envelope** [ˈɛnvəˌlop] 名 信封

There is no stamp in this *envelope*.

這個信封上沒有郵票。

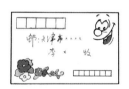

**equal** [ˈikwəl] 形 相等的,均等的

Divide the cake into four *equal* parts.

把這個蛋糕分成四等份。

**eraser** [ɪˈresɚ] 名 橡皮擦

I haven't an *eraser*.

我沒有橡皮擦。

**error** ['ɛrɚ] 名 錯誤

There is a spelling *error* in this word.
這個單詞裏有一個拼寫錯誤。

**escalator** ['ɛskə,letɚ] 名 自動樓梯

The *escalator* is working.
自動樓梯正在運行。

**escape** [ə'skep,ɛ'skep] 動 逃跑

The monkey has *escaped* from the cage.
猴子已經從籠子裏逃了出來。

**Europe** ['jʊrəp] 名 歐洲

He will visit some countries in *Europe*.
他將要訪問一些歐洲國家。

**even** ['ivən] 副 甚至

*Even* children know this.
連小孩都懂得這點。

**evening** ['ivnɪŋ] 名 晚上

Mary listens to music on Sunday *evening*.
瑪麗在星期天晚上聽音樂。

**ever** ['ɛvɚ] 副 曾經

Have you *ever* been to Taipei?
你曾經去過台北嗎？

**every** ['ɛv(ə)rɪ] 形 每一的，每個的

The old woman takes a walk *every* morning.
那個老人每天早上都去散步。

注
every, each 的區別: every 只作形容詞，
用於三個或三個以上的場合，強調整體
或全體; each 可作形容詞和代詞，用於
兩個或兩個以上的場合，強調個體。

## everybody ['ɛvrɪˌbɑdɪ,'ɛvrɪˌbʌdɪ] 代 每人，人人

*Everybody* stands up.
每個人都站起來了。
everyone = everybody

## everything ['ɛvrɪˌθɪŋ] 代 每件事，事事

Money is not *everything*.
金錢不是萬能的。

## examination [ɪgˌzæməˈneʃən] 名 檢查，考試

He passed the *examination*.
他考試及格了。

## except [ɪkˈsɛpt] 介 除……之外

Everyone hand in their homework *except* you.
除你之外每個人都把作業交上來了。

## exciting [ɪkˈsaɪtɪŋ] 形 令人興奮的，使人激動的

This is so *exciting*.
這是如此的令人興奮。

## excuse [ɪkˈskjuz,ɪkˈskɪuz] 動 原諒，寬恕

*Excuse* me!
請原諒！（對不起！）

## exercise ['ɛksɚˌsaɪz] 名 練習

Did you do last night's math *exercise*?
你做了昨晚的數學作業了嗎？

動 鍛鍊

I *exercise* three times each week.
我每周鍛鍊三次。

exercise-book 練習本

## exit ['ɛgzɪt,'ɛksɪt] 名 出口

Go out the main *exit*.
從正門出去。

## expect [ɪk'spɛkt] 動 盼望、期望

We *expect* that it will rain today.

我們盼望著今天下雨。

## expensive [ɪk'spɛnsɪv] 形 昂貴的

He didn't buy the *expensive* car.

他沒買那輛昂貴的汽車。

## explain [ɪk'splen] 動 解釋、說明

The teacher *explained* the problem to me.

老師向我解釋了那個問題。

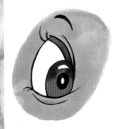

## eye [aɪ] 名 眼睛

We should keep our *eyes* well.

我們應該保護好我們的眼睛。

eyeball 眼球；　eyebrow 眉毛

# F f

**ace** [fes] 名 臉
Go and wash your *face*.
去洗洗你的臉。

**act** [fækt] 名 事實
She told her parents all the *facts*.
她把全部事實告訴了她父母。

**factory** ['fækt(ə)rɪ] 名 工廠
The car is made in that *factory*.
這輛汽車是由那家工廠生產出來的。

**fail** [fel] 動 ①不及格 ②失敗
① Helen *failed* her math examination.
海倫數學考試不及格。
② His plan has *failed*.
他的計劃失敗了。

**fair** [fɛr,fær] 形 公平的,合理的
That's not *fair*.
那是不公平的。

**fairy** ['fɛrɪ,'færɪ] 名 仙女,精靈
I was a *fairy* for Halloween.
我是萬聖節的一個精靈。

**fall** [fɔl] 動 跌落,落下
His bag *fell* into the river.
他的書包掉到了河裏。
反 rise 升起

lamp 燈

fireplace 壁爐

fire 火

telephone 電話

globe 地球儀

carpet 地毯

book 書

**family** ['fæm(ə)lɪ] 名 家庭
I have a large *family*.
我生活在一個大家庭裏。

**famous** ['feməs] 形 著名的，出名的
Does Mary want to be a *famous* dancer?
瑪麗想成爲一名著名舞蹈家嗎？

**fan** [fæn] 名 扇子，電風扇
Kate wants to *turn* on the *fan*.
凱特想打開電風扇。

**far** [fɑr] 副 遠，遙遠地
How *far* is it to your house?
到你家有多遠？
反 near 近，附近

**fare** [fɛr, fær] 名 車費，船費
What is the train *fare* to Taipei?
去台北的火車票是多少錢？

**farm** [fɑrm] 名 農場，農莊
We'll go and visit the *farm*.
我們將去訪問那個農場。

**farmer** ['fɑrmə-] 名 農民，農場主
The *farmer* is driving a tractor.
那個農民正在開拖拉機。

**fast** [fæst] 形 快的，迅速的
Mike wants to ride a *fast* horse.
邁克想騎一匹快馬。
反 slow 慢的
副 快，迅速地
Don't read so *fast*.
不要讀得這麼快。
反 slowly 慢慢地

**fasten**  ['fæsn] 動 紮牢，扣住
Peter is *fastening* his belt.
彼得正在扣安全帶。

**fat**  [fæt] 形 胖的
Billy is a *fat* boy.
比利是個胖男孩。
反　thin 瘦的

**father**  ['faðɚ] 名 父親
My *father* isn't in.
我父親不在家。

**fault**  [fɔlt] 名 錯誤
It's my *fault*, Dad.
爸爸,是我錯了。

**favorite**  ['fev(ə)rɪt] 形 最喜愛的，最中意的
What's your *favorite* song?
你最喜歡什麼歌曲？

**fear**  [fɪr] 動 害怕，畏懼
I *fear* the cold.
我怕冷。

**feather**  ['fɛðɚ] 名 羽毛
What a beautiful *feather*!
多麼美麗的羽毛啊！

**February**  ['fɛbrʊ,ɛrɪ] 名 二月
Spring begins in *February*.
春天從二月份開始。

**feed**  [fid] 動 餵養，飼養
Kate *feeds* her cat every day.
凱特每天都給貓餵食。

**feel**  [fil] 動 感覺
How do you *feel* today?
你今天感覺怎麼樣？

migratory bird
侯鳥

nest
鳥巢

rooster
公雞

macaw
金剛鸚鵡

quail
鵪鶉

sparrow
麻雀

robin
知更鳥

bluebird
藍色知更鳥

turkey
火雞

swan
天鵝

swallow
燕子

mandarin
鴛鴦

owl
貓頭鷹

pheasant
雉雞

chick
小雞

hen
母雞

parrot
鸚鵡

eagle
老鷹

peacock
孔雀

buzzard
禿鷹

pigeon
鴿子

cardinal
北美紅雀

goose
鵝

71

**fence** [fɛns] 名 栅欄，籬笆

There's a *fence* around the school.
校園四周圍著柵欄。

**festival** ['fɛstəvl] 名 節日

There are many important *festivals* in China.
中國有許多重要的節日。

中國的主要節日

New Year's Day 元旦；Spring Festival 春節；

Lantern Festival 元宵節；Dragon-Boat Festival 端午節；

Children's Day 國際兒童節；Mid-Autumn Festival 中秋節；

Teacher's Day 教師節；National Day 國慶節

**fetch** [fɛtʃ] 動 去取來

The dog *fetched* a bone.
狗叼來一根骨頭。

**fever** ['fivɚ] 名 發燒

Does Tom have a *fever*?
湯姆發燒嗎？

**few** [fju,fɪu] 形 少數的，不多的

*Few* people know about it.
幾乎沒有什麼人知道這一點。

A *few* people know about it.
有幾個人知道這一點。

比較

few 表示否定意義，a few 表示肯定意義。

**field** [fild] 名 田野，田地

Don't walk in the *field*.
不要在田地裏行走。

**fifteen** ['fɪftɪn,ˌfɪf'tin] 數 十五

I'll be *fifteen* in two days.
再過兩天我就 15 歲了。

**fifty** ['fɪftɪ] 名 五十

There are *fifty* pupils in our class.
我們班有50名學生。

**fight** [faɪt] 動 打架

Tom and Dick *fought* yesterday.
湯姆和迪克昨天打架了。

**fill** [fɪl] 動 充滿，填滿

Please *fill* the glass with milk.
請往玻璃杯裏倒滿牛奶。

**film** [fɪlm] 名 ①電影 ②底片
① I enjoy this *film* very much.
   我非常欣賞這部電影。
② I'll buy a roll of color *film*.
   我要買一卷彩色底片。

**find** [faɪnd] 動 找到

Did you *find* your green shirt?
你找到你的綠襯衫了嗎？

反 lose 失去

**fine** [faɪn] 形 ①美好的，健康的 ②晴朗的
① How are you? — *Fine*, thank you.
   你好嗎？—很好，謝謝你。
② It's a *fine* day.
   今天天氣很好。

名 罰金

David paid a *fine* for parking in the wrong place.
因爲沒按指定位置停車，所以大衛受到了處罰。

**finger** ['fɪŋɚ] 名 手指
Count your *fingers*.
數一下你的手指。

## finish ['fɪnɪʃ] 動 完成，結束

Rose *finished* her homework.
羅絲做完了作業。
反　begin　開始

## fire ['faɪr] 名 火，火災

Keep away from the *fire*!
勿靠近火場!
fire engine　消防車
fireman　消防員

## fireworks ['faɪr,wɜks] 名 煙花，煙火

The *fireworks* are beautiful.
煙火非常好看。

## first [fɜst] 數 第一

He won the *first* place in the game.
他在這次比賽中，得了第一名。

副 首先，最初
The duck arrived *first*.
這隻鴨子第一個到達了。
反　last　最後

## fish [fɪʃ] 名 魚

*Fish* live in the water.
魚生活在水中。
注
fish是可數名詞，但單複數形式相同，如: a fish(一條魚)，　two fish
(兩條魚) 作魚肉講時，是不可數名詞，無複數形式。
複數 fishes 則表示不同種類的魚。

## fisherman ['fɪʃə·mən] 名 漁民

The *fisherman* is catching fish.
那位漁民正在捕魚。

## fit [fɪt] 動 適合，符合

The shirt doesn't *fit* Tom.
湯姆穿這件襯衫不合身。

**five** [faɪv] 數 五.
There are *five* pens in this box.
這個盒子裏有5支鋼筆。

**fix** [fɪks] 動 修理
The man is *fixing* the TV.
那個人正在修理電視機。

**flag** [flæg] 名 旗
This is our national *flag*. 這是我們的國旗。

**flame** [flem] 名 火焰
The color of *flame* is fair.
火焰的顏色是白皙明亮的。

**flat** [flæt] 形 平的，扁平的
My bicycle tire is *flat*.
我的腳踏車胎沒氣了。

**float** [flot] 動 漂浮，浮動
Wood can *float* on water.
木頭能浮在水面上。

**flood** [flʌd] 名 洪水，水災
Many fields were covered in that *flood*.
在那次水災中，許多田地被淹沒。

**floor** [flor,flɔr] 名 地板
Lucy is playing on the *floor*.
露茜正在地板上玩耍。

**flour** ['flaʊr] 名 麵粉
Bread is made from *flour*.
麵包是由麵粉做成的。

**flower** ['flaʊɚ,flaʊr] 名 花
Peter gave his mother a bunch of *flowers*.
彼得送給媽媽一束花。
flowerbed 花壇

**flu** ['flu,flɪu] 名 流行性感冒
I had the *flu* last winter.
去年冬天我患了流行性感冒。

**flute** [flut,flɪut] 名 長笛
She can play the *flute*.
她會吹笛子。

**fly** [flaɪ] 動 飛行
Eagles *fly* very high.
鷹飛得非常高。

名 蒼蠅
There was a *fly* on your rice.
你的米飯上有一隻蒼蠅。

**foam** [fom] 名 泡沫
There was an inch of *foam* in my glass.
我的杯子裏冒出了一英吋的泡沫。

**fold** [fold] 動 折疊
*Fold* it like this. 像這樣折疊

**follow** ['falo,'falə] 動 跟隨
Jim *followed* Mike up the hill.
吉姆跟著麥克爬上了山。

**food** [fud] 名 食物
We eat many kinds of *food*.
我們吃各種各樣的食物。

**foolish** ['fulɪʃ] 形 傻的、愚蠢的
Don't be *foolish*! 別傻了!

**foot** [fʊt] 名 ①腳 ②英呎
① Tom is pointing at his left *foot*.
湯姆正指著他的左腳。
② This tree is twenty *feet* high.
這棵樹有二十英呎高。

**for** [fɔr,弱 fɚ] 介 ①爲了，給　②累計，達
① Sandy, this egg is *for* you.
桑迪，這顆雞蛋是給你的。
② He worked *for* a whole day.
他工作了一整天。

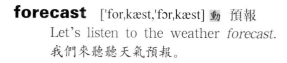

**F**

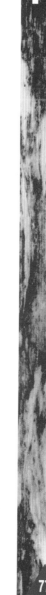

**forecast** ['fɔr,kæst,'fɔr,kæst] 動　預報
Let's listen to the weather *forecast*.
我們來聽聽天氣預報。

**forehead** ['fɔrɪd,'fɑrɪd,'fɔr,hɛd] 名　前額
Look at Lucy's *forehead*.
看看露茜的前額。

**forest** ['fɔrɪst,'fɑrɪst] 名 森林
The *forest* was on fire.
森林著火了。

**forget** [fɚ'gɛt] 動 忘記
He always *forgets* little things.
他總是忘記一些小事情。
反　remember 記得

**fork** [fɔrk] 名 叉子
Can you use a *fork*?
你會用叉子嗎?

**forty** ['fɔtɪ] 數 四十
Read the number *forty* in Chinese.
用中文讀出 40 這個數。

**forward** ['fɔrwɚd] 介 向前
I look *forward* to seeing you again.
我期望再次見到你。
Move *forward* carefully. 小心翼翼往前走。

**four** [for,fɔr] 數 四
Can you eat *four* eggs?
你能吃掉四個鷄蛋嗎?

**fourteen** ['for'tin,fɔr'tin] 數 十四
Mary is *fourteen*. 瑪麗14歲了。

**fox** [fɑks] 名 狐狸
A *fox* has a thick tail.
狐狸有一條粗尾巴。

**France** [fræns] 名 法國
This is the flag of *France*.
這是法國國旗。

**free** [fri] 形 ①有空的 ②免費的
① Are you *free* on Saturday?
星期六你有空嗎?
② There's a *free* film tonight.
今晚有一場免費電影。

**freezing** ['friziŋ] 形 凍結的
It's sometimes *freezing* in winter.
冬天有時候結冰。

**French** [frɛntʃ] 形 法國的
He is from *French*.
他來自法國。

名 法語
They speak *French* very well.
他們的法語講得非常棒。

**fresh** [frɛʃ] 形 新鮮的
I drink *fresh* milk every morning.
每天早上我都喝鮮牛奶。

**Friday** ['fraɪdɪ] 名 星期五
The students go home on *Friday*.
學生們星期五回家。

**friend** [frɛnd] 名 朋友
Who is your best *friend*?
誰是你最好的朋友?

### friendly ['frɛndlɪ] 形 友好的

The children here are *friendly* with one another.

這裏的孩子彼此之間十分友好。

### frisby ['frɪzbɪ] 名 飛盤

Throw the *frisby* like this.

像這樣扔飛盤。

### frog [frɑg,frɔg] 名 青蛙

A *frog* has four legs.

青蛙有四條腿。

### from [frɑm,弱 frəm] 介 ①從 ②來自

① Mr. White works *from* morning till night.

懷特先生從早到晚工作。

② Who comes *from* America?

誰是美國人?

### front [frʌnt] 形 前面的

There's a blackboard on the *front* wall.

前面牆上有一塊黑板。

### rown [fraʊn] 名 皺眉

Why do you have a *frown* on your face?

你為什麼皺眉頭呢?

### ruit [fr(ɪ)ut] 名 水果

*Fruit* and vegetables are good for us.

水果和蔬菜對於我們大家來說很有好處。

### fry [fraɪ] 動 油炸,油煎

The cook is *frying* fish for dinner.

那個廚師正在為晚餐煎魚。

### full [fʊl] 形 滿的,充滿……的

The bus is *full*.

公共汽車裏擠滿了人。

**funny**  ['fʌnɪ] 形 有趣的，可笑的
   It looks funny when Diana puts her father's coat on.
   戴安娜穿上她父親的上衣時，看上去很可笑。

**furniture**  ['fɜnɪtʃɚ] 名 家俱
   All the *furniture* is new.
   所有的家俱都是新的。

**future**  ['fjutʃɚ,fɪutʃɚ] 名 將來，未來
   What will happen in the *future*?
   將來會發生什麼事呢？

**game** [gem] 名 遊戲

Let's play a *game* of musical chairs.
我們玩搶椅子的遊戲吧。

**garage** [gə'raʒ,gə'radʒ,gæraʒ] 名 車庫

David is driving his car into his *garage*.
大衛正在把車開進車庫。

**garbage** ['garbɪdʒ] 名 垃圾

Keep the *garbage* in the garbage can.
把垃圾扔進垃圾筒裏。

garbage can 垃圾筒

**garden** ['gardn̩] 名 花園

They are playing in the *garden*.
他們正在花園裏玩。

**gardener** ['gardnɚ] 名 園丁

The *gardener* is working outside.
那個園丁正在室外工作。

**gas** [gæs] 名 氣體，煤氣

Diana has a *gas* oven.
戴安娜有一個煤氣爐。

### gate [get] 名 大門

The city *gate* is closed.

城門關閉著。

### gather ['gæðɚ] 動 聚集

The children *gathered* around the teacher.

孩子們圍著那個老師。

### gentleman ['dʒɛntlmən] 名 男士，先生

Ladies and *gentlemen*！

女士們，先生們!

### geography [dʒi'ɑgrəfɪ] 名 地理

Tom likes learning about *geography*.

湯姆喜歡了解地理知識。

### German ['dʒɝmən] 形 德國的，德國人的

Is this a *German* car?

這是一輛德國造的汽車嗎?

名 德語，德國人

I don't speak *German*. 我不講德語。

### Germany ['dʒɝmənɪ] 名 德國

Has David been to *Germany*? 大衛去過德國嗎?

### gesture ['dʒɛstʃɚ] 名 手勢

Different *gestures* have different meanings.

不同的手勢代表不同的意義。

### get [gɛt] 動 得到，買到

Billy *got* a chocolate car.

比利得到一輛巧克力汽車。

*Get* me a new bag, mum.

媽媽，給我買一個新背包吧!

get on 上車; get off 下車;

get to 到達; get up 起床

**ghost** [gost] 名 鬼

*Ghost* stories scare me.

鬼故事使我非常害怕。

**giant** [dʒɑɪənt] 名 巨人

The *giant* in the fairy tale is foolish.

童話中那個巨人是很愚蠢的。

**gift** [gɪft] 名 禮物

Billy got many birthday *gifts*.

比利得到許多生日禮物。

**girl** [gɝl] 名 女孩

Alice is a kind *girl*.

艾麗斯是個善良的女孩。

**give** [gɪv] 動 給

*Give* the apple to me, please.

請把那個蘋果給我。

**glad** [glæd] 形 高興的

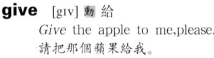

I'm very *glad* to see you.

見到你很高興。

反 sad 悲傷的

**glare** [glɛr, glær] 動 瞪著眼

They are *glaring* at each other.

他們怒目而視。

**glass** [glæs] 名 ①玻璃 ②玻璃杯

① *Glass* is hard and smooth.

玻璃不但堅硬而且光滑。

② There are three *glasses* on the table.

桌子上有3個玻璃杯。

**glasses** ['glæsɪs] 名 眼鏡

Jane often wears *glasses*.

珍經常戴著眼鏡。

### glove [glʌv] 名 手套
He is catching fish with his *gloves*.
他戴著手套釣魚。

### glue [gl(ı)ʊ] 名 膠水
Can I borrow your *glue*?
我可以借用你的膠水嗎?

## go [go] 動 去
The children *go* to school early.
孩子們去學校很早。
go camping 去露營; go fishing 去釣魚;

go skating 去滑冰; go swimming 去游泳

## goal [gol] 名 目標,射門
I made three *goals* in last night's game.
在昨晚的比賽中我3次擊中目標。

## goat [got] 名 山羊
*Goats* can climb well. 山羊爬山非常敏捷。

## God [gɑd] 名 上帝
Do you believe in *God* ?
你信仰上帝嗎?

## gold [gold] 名 金子,黃金
*Gold* costs a lot of money.
黃金非常值錢。

形 含金的,金制的
Do you have a *gold* watch?
你有一個金錶嗎?

### golden ['goldn] 形 金黃色的
Kate's hair is *golden* blonde.
凱特留著一頭金髮。

### goldfish ['gold,fiʃ] 名 金魚
Do you like *goldfish*?
你喜歡金魚嗎?

**good** [gʊd] 形 好的

He has a *good* father.

他有一個好父親。

Good morning! 早上好!　Good afternoon! 下午好!

Good evening! 晚上好!　Good night! 晚安!

**goodbye** [gʊd'baɪ] 嘆 再見

Mary said *goodbye* to her mother.

瑪麗向媽媽說了聲再見。

**goose** [gus] 名 鵝

A *goose* is larger than a duck.

鵝比鴨子大。

**gossip** ['gɑsəp] 名 愛說閒話的人

We don't like a *gossip*.

我們不喜歡愛說閒話的人。

**grade** [gred] 名 年級

Peter is in *Grade 5*.

彼得在五年級。

**grandfather** ['græn(d).fɑðɚ] 名（外）祖父，爺爺

Tom's *grandfather* was a gardener.

湯姆的祖父是個園丁。

**grandmother** ['græn(d),mʌðɚ] 名（外）祖母，奶奶

His *grandmother* is seventy.

他的奶奶70歲了。

**grape** [grep] 名 葡萄

They are picking *grapes*.

他們在摘葡萄。

**grass** [græs] 名 草，草地

Keep off the *grass*!

勿踐踏草地!

**grave** [grev] 形 嚴肅的，嚴重的
You look so *grave*. What's wrong?
你看起來這麼嚴肅，發生了什麼事？

**gray** [gre] 形 (美)
**grey** [gre] 形 (英) 灰色的
The *elephant* is grey.
這頭大象是灰色的。

**great** [gret] 形 ①偉大的，巨大的 ②擅長，精於
① There are many *great* men in the world.
世界上有許多偉人。
② I was *great* on the math test.
我擅長數學考試。

**Greece** [gris] 名 希臘
Have you heard something about *Greece*?
你聽到過一些有關希臘的事情嗎？

**Greek** [grik] 名 希臘人，希臘語
I don't think you can speak *Greek*.
我想你不會講希臘語。

**greedy** [gridı] 形 貪吃的，貪婪的
Don't be *greedy*. Save some
food for the others.
別貪吃，給其他人留一些食物。

**green** [grin] 形 綠色的
Grass is *green*.
草是綠色的。

**greengrocer** ['grin,grosə] 名
蔬菜水果商
Betty's grandfather is a *greengrocer*.
貝蒂的祖父是個蔬菜水果商人。

**greet** [grit] 動 歡迎，迎接

Peter and Lucy *greeted* their grandmother
with a bunch of flowers.
彼得和露西帶了一束花去迎接奶奶。

**grocer** ['grosə] 名 雜貨商，食品商

Jim got some sugar from the *grocer*.
吉姆從那家食品店裏買了些糖。

**G**

**ground** [graʊnd] 名 地面

The baby is sitting on the *ground*.
那個嬰兒正坐在地上。

**group** [grup] 名 群，組

They are building a *group*
of new houses.
他們正在興建一片新房子。

**grow** [gro] 動 ①生長，長大　②種植

① The tree *grows* well.
　這棵樹長得很好。

② The farmer *grows* carrots in his field.
　那個農民在地裏種胡蘿蔔。

**grown-up** ['gron,ʌp] 名 成年人（與小孩相對而言）

Some films are only for *grown-ups*.
有些電影只適合成年人看。

**guard** [gɑrd] 名 士兵

The *guard* is standing at the gate.
那個士兵正站在大門口。

**guess** [gɛs] 動 猜

*Guess* how old I am.
猜猜我多大了。

**guest** [gɛst] 名 客人

Mary opened the door for the *guests*.
瑪麗給客人們開了門。

## guide [gaɪd] 名 嚮導，導遊

The *guide* told us an interesting story.
導遊向我們講了一個有趣的故事。

## guitar [gɪ'tɑr] 名 吉他

David likes playing the *guitar*.
大衛喜歡彈吉他。

## gun [gʌn] 名 槍

Every policeman has a *gun*.
每個警察都有一支槍。

## gym [dʒɪm] 名 ①體育館　②體育課

① The children do exercise in the *gym*.
　孩子們在體育館鍛鍊。
② They like *gym* class.
　他們喜歡體育課。

# H h

**habit**  ['hæbɪt] 名 習慣
Smoking is a bad *habit*.
抽煙是一種壞習慣。

**hair**  [hɛr,hær] 名 頭髮
Sue's *hair* is short.
蘇留著短髮

**haircut**  ['hɛr,kʌt, 'hær,kʌt] 名 剪髮，髮型
Betty got a *haircut*.
貝蒂變換了髮型。

**half**  [hæf] 名 一半
*Half* of the cake is enough.
半塊蛋糕就足夠了。

**hall**  [hɔl] 名 大廳
Leave your coat in the *hall*, please.
請把外套留在大廳裏。

**ham**  [hæm] 名 火腿
This is a juicy *ham*.
這是一根多汁的火腿。

**hamburger**  ['hæmbɝgɚ] 名 漢堡
Mike likes *hamburgers*.
邁克喜歡吃漢堡。

## hammer ['hæmɚ] 名 鐵錘，榔頭

Pass me a *hammer*.
遞給我一把榔頭。

## hand [hænd] 名 手

My *hands* are clean.
我的手是乾淨的。

## handkerchief ['hæŋkɚtʃɪf, 'hæŋkɚˌtʃɪf] 名 手帕

Kate has a red *handkerchief*.
凱特有一塊紅手帕。

## handle ['hændl] 名 柄，把手

Can you see the *handle* of the door?
你看見門的把手了嗎？

## handsome ['hænsəm] 形 英俊的，好看的

The actor is very *handsome*.
那名男演員非常英俊。

## hang [hæŋ] 動 懸掛

Betty is *hanging* her clothes.
貝蒂正在掛她的衣服。

## happen ['hæpən] 動 發生

What has *happened*?
發生了什麼事？

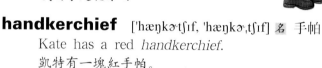

## happy ['hæpɪ] 形 快樂的

*Happy* birthday to you!
祝你生日快樂！

## hard [hɑrd] 形 困難的,堅硬的

This is a *hard* question.
這是一道難題。
A stone is *hard*.
石頭是堅硬的。
反 soft 柔軟的

**H**

**hare** [hɛr, hær] 名 野兔
The farmer caught a *hare*.
農夫逮著了一隻野兔。

**has** [hæz, 弱 həz, əz] 動 have 的第三人稱單數現在式

**have** [hæv, 弱 həv, əv] 動 有
Lucy *has* a green balloon.
露茜有一個綠氣球。
She *have* a story book.
她有一本故事書。
I *has* a car.
我有一輛小汽車。

**hat** [hæt] 名 帽子
This *hat* is too big for her.
這頂帽子太大了，她戴不了。

**hatch** [hætʃ] 動 孵，孵出
Did the eggs *hatch* yet?
小雞孵出來了嗎?

**hate** [het] 動 憎恨，討厭
John *hates* dogs.
約翰討厭狗。

**he** [hi, 弱 hɪ, ɪ] 代 他
*He* has a ball.
他有一個球。
*He* said so himself.
他自己這樣說的。

**head** [hɛd] 名 頭
The rock fell and hit him on the *head*.
石頭掉下來，砸著他的頭。

**headache** ['hɛd,ek] 名 頭痛
She has a bad *headache*.
她頭痛得厲害。

### headmaster ['hɛd'mæstɚ] 名 校長
This is our *headmaster*, Mr. Wang.
這是我們的王校長。

### headmistress ['hɛd'mɪstrɪs] 名 女校長
Their *headmistress* is Mrs. Li.
他們的校長是李女士。

### health [hɛlθ] 名 健康
How is your *health*?
你的健康狀況怎樣？

### healthy ['hɛlθɪ] 形 健康的
Exercises can make us *healthy*.
鍛鍊能使我們健康。

### hear [hɪr] 動 聽
Can you *hear* me?
你能聽見我說話嗎？

### heart [hɑrt] 名 心
I can feel my *heart* beating.
我能感覺到我的心跳。

### heat [hit] 名 熱
The sun gives off *heat* and light.
太陽散發出光和熱。

動 加熱
Mom,please *heat* up the soup for me.
媽媽、請為我熱一下湯。

### heavy ['hɛvɪ] 形 重的
Sandy's schoolbag is *heavy*.
桑迪的書包很重。
反 light 輕的

### height [haɪt] 名 高度
Do you know the *height* of this building?
你知道這座大樓有多高嗎？

**hello** [hɛ'lo, hə'lo, 'hʌlo] 嘆 喂（用於打招
呼，引起注意）
"*Hello*, Mr. White." "你好，懷特先生。"
"*Hello*, Sandy." "你好，桑迪。"

**helicopter** ['hɛlɪ'kɑptɚ, 'hilɪ,kɑptɚ] 名
直昇飛機
Who's in the *helicopter*?
誰在直昇飛機裏面？

**helmet** ['hɛlmɪt] 名 盔，鋼盔
The brick dropped on his *helmet*.
磚頭砸在他的頭盔上。

**help** [hɛlp] 動 幫助
Let me *help* you.
讓我來幫你吧。

**hen** [hɛn] 名 母雞
A *hen* lays eggs.
母雞會下蛋。

**here** [hɪr] 副 在這兒，在這裏
Put your bag *here*.
把你的書包放在這裏。
反 there 在那裏

**hi** [haɪ] 嘆 喂（表示問候，相當於 hello）
*Hi*, Mike! 你好，邁克!

**hide** [haɪd] 動 躲避，藏
Let's play *hide* and seek.
我們來玩捉迷藏吧。
hide and seek 捉迷藏

**high** [haɪ] 形 高的
How *high* can you jump?
你能跳多高?
反 low 低的

**hike**  [haɪk] 動 徒步旅行
They are *hiking* around the lake.
他們正繞著湖徒步旅行。

**hill**  [hɪl] 名 小山
John lives at the foot of the *hill*.
約翰居住在小山腳下。

**hit**  [hɪt] 動 打，擊
Can you catch it, if I *hit* the ball?
如果我擊球，你能接住嗎？

**hobby**  ['habɪ] 名 愛好
Alice's *hobby* is taking picture.
艾麗斯的愛好是攝影。

**hold**  [hold] 動 握住，拿著
Can you *hold* this toy for me?
你能替我拿著這個玩具嗎？

**hole**  [hol] 名 洞，孔
The hare ran into its *hole*.
那隻野兔鑽進它的洞裏去了。

**holiday**  ['halə,de] 名 假日
We don't work on *holidays*.
我們在假日裏不工作。

**home**  [hom] 名 家
I think Jim is at *home*.
我想吉姆在家。

比較

family, house, home: family 指家庭成員；house 指居住的建築物本

身而言；home 指強調某人出生及撫育其長大的那種環境地點。

**homework**  ['hom,wɜk] 名 家庭作業
After dinner, they do their *homework*.
晚飯後，他們做家庭作業。

**honest** ['ɑnɪst] 形 誠實的
We like *honest* men.
我們喜歡誠實的人。

**honey** ['hʌnɪ] 名 蜂蜜
There's not much *honey*
in the cupboard.
碗櫥裏沒有多少蜂蜜了。

H

**hook** [hʊk] 名 鈎
Jane hang her bag on the *hook*.
珍把她的書包掛在勾子上。

**hoop** [hʊp] 名 圈，鐵環
The dog jumped through the *hoop*.
那隻狗從鐵環中跳了過去。

**hop** [hɑp] 動 單足跳躍
Look, the boy is *hopping*.
看，那個男孩正在單腳跳躍。

**hope** [hop] 動 希望
I *hope* that it will be fine tomorrow.
我希望明天是個好天氣。

名 希望
There is no *hope* of winning.
沒有獲勝的希望。

**hopscotch** ['hɑp,skɑtʃ] 名 跳房子，遊戲
*Hopscotch* is a girls' game.
跳房子遊戲是女孩子們的遊戲。

**horn** [hɔrn] 名 角
Some animals have *horns*.
有些動物長角。

**horse** [hɔrs] 名 馬
*Horses* can run fast.
馬能跑得很快。

95

## hospital ['hɑspɪtl] 名 醫院
Mike is in *hospital*.
邁克住院了。

## hot [hɑt] 形 熱的
It's very *hot* today.
今天非常熱。

## hot dog 熱狗
*Hot dogs* are good with mustard.
放芥末的熱狗好吃。

## hotel [ho'tɛl] 名 旅館
This is a big *hotel*.
這是一家大旅館。

## hour [aʊr] 名 小時
There are twenty-four *hours* in a day
一天有二十四個小時。

## house [haʊs] 名 房子
Your *house* is beautiful.
你的房子很漂亮。

## housewife ['haʊs,waɪf] 名 家庭主婦
Diana is a *housewife*.
戴安娜是個家庭主婦。

## housework ['haʊs,wɜk] 名 家務
She does her *housework* every day.
她每天都做家務。

## how [haʊ] 副 怎樣，如何
"*How* do you go to school?" "By bike."
"你怎樣去上學？" "騎腳踏車。"
*How* are you?
你好嗎？
*How* do you do?
你好嗎？（初次見面時問候語）

**H**

**however** [hɑʊˈɛvɚ] 副 無論如何

*However* tired you may be, you must do it.
不管你多累，你都必須做。

**hug** [hʌg] 動 擁抱

Mother *hugs* Kate when she comes
home from school.
凱特從學校回來時，媽媽總是抱她一下。

**hundred** [ˈhʌndrəd, ˈhʌndrɪd] 名 百

Father gave Betty one *hundred* dollars.
父親給了貝蒂一百美元。

**hungry** [ˈhʌŋgrɪ] 形 饑餓的

The children are *hungry*.
孩子們餓了。

**hunt** [hʌnt] 動 打獵

I like to *hunt* for hares.
我喜歡打野兔。

**hunter** [ˈhʌntɚ] 名 獵人

The *hunter* walked slowly
through the woods.
獵人慢慢地走過樹林。

**hurray** [həˈrɔ, həˈrɑ, hʊrɔ] 嘆 好哇

Hip, hip, *hurray!*
好哇，好哇，好哇！

**hurry** [ˈhɝɪ] 動 匆忙，趕快

*Hurry* up, children! 快點，孩子們！

**hurt** [hɝt] 動 傷害，疼痛

Mary *hurt* her feet when she jumped.
瑪麗跳時弄傷了腳。

**husband** [ˈhʌzbənd] 名 丈夫

They are *husband* and wife.
他們是夫妻。

**I**

**I** [aɪ] 代 我
*I'*m Mike.
我叫邁克。
*I* walk to school by myself.
我自己走著去學校。

**ice** [aɪs] 名 冰
Peter is skating on the *ice*.
彼得正在冰上滑冰。

**ice cream** 冰淇淋

**idea** [aɪ'diə, aɪ'dɪə] 名 主意，辦法
I have a good *idea*.
我有一個好主意。

**idle** ['aɪdl] 形 懶散的，沒事做的
Don't be an *idle* child.
不要做個懶散的孩子。

**if** [ɪf] 連 ①假如，如果　②是否
① *If* you have questions, you
　　can ask me.
　　如果你有問題的話，你可以來問我。
② Jane doesn't know *if* he can
　　help her.
　　珍不知道他是否會幫助她。

**ill** [ɪl] 形 病的

John is *ill*. 約翰病了。

反　well 健康的

同　sick 病的

**illness** [ˈɪlnɪs] 名 病，疾病

He can't work because of his *illness*.
因爲他病了，所以他不能工作。

**imagine** [ɪˈmædʒɪn] 動 想像

Tom *imagines* himself as a policeman.
湯姆想像自己是一名警察。

**important** [ɪmˈpɔrtnt] 形 重要的

It's *important* to me.
對我來説,那很重要。

**in** [ɪn] 介 在……裏，在……内

There is some water *in* the glass.
玻璃杯裏有一些水。

副 在家裏

Come *in*. Dad is in.　進來，爸爸在家。

反　out 在外面

**inch** [ɪntʃ] 名 英吋

This line is fifteen *inches*.
這根線有15英吋。

**indeed** [ɪnˈdid, ņˈdɪd] 副 確實，實在

Thank you very much *indeed*!
實在是非常感謝!

**Indian** [ˈɪndɪən, ˈɪndjən] 名 印度人，印第安人

They are *Indians*.
她們是印第安人（印度人）。

形 印度的

I like to see *Indian* films.
我喜歡看印度電影。

### ink [ɪŋk] 名 墨水
This is a bottle of *ink*.
這是一瓶墨水。

### insect ['ɪnsɛkt] 名 昆蟲
Come and see the *insects*.
來看看這些昆蟲。

### inside ['ɪn'saɪd, 'ɪnˌsaɪd] 介 在……裏面
The little boy is *inside* the house.
小男孩在屋子裏面。
反 outside 在……外面

### inspector [ɪn'spɛktə] 名 視察員
The *inspectors* have come.
視察員們已經來了。

### instead [ɪn'stɛd] 副 代替
Sandy took Dad's tea *instead* of his orange.
桑迪拿了爸爸的茶，而不是他自己的橘子汁。

### interesting ['ɪnt(ə)rɪstɪŋ, 'ɪntəˌrɛstɪn] 形 有趣的
Rose is reading an *interesting* book.
羅絲正在讀一本有趣的書。

### into [母音前 'ɪntʊ, 子音前 'ɪntə] 介 進入……之內
Those men are going *into* the hole.
那些人正在進那個洞。

### introduce [ˌɪntrə'djʊs, ˌɪntrə'd(ɪ)ʊs] 動 介紹
Let me *introduce* myself. 讓我來自我介紹一下。

### invent [ɪn'vɛnt] 動 發明
Who *invented* the steam engine?
誰發明了蒸汽機。

### invite [ɪn'vaɪt] 動 邀請
Alice *invited* the Toms to her party.
艾麗斯邀請湯姆一家人參加她的晚會。

**iron** [ˈaɪɚn] 名 ①鐵 ②熨斗

① The gate is made of *iron*.
這座大門是鐵製成的。

② Mary is ironing her dress with an electric *iron*.
瑪麗正在用電熨斗燙她的裙子。

**island** [ˈaɪlənd] 名 島，島嶼

No one lives on the island.
那個島上無人居住。

**it** [ɪt] 代 它

*It* is a clever dog.
它是一條聰明的狗。

Look after *it* carefully.
仔細照顧著它。

Now *it* can stand up itself.
現在它能自己站立起來了。

**Italian** [ɪˈtæljən, əˈtæljən] 名 義大利人

The actress is an *Italian*.
那名女演員是義大利人。

形 義大利的

That's an *Italian* car.
那輛車是義大利製造的。

**Italy** [ˈɪtl̩ɪ] 名 義大利

Who comes from *Italy*?
誰是義大利人？

**itch** [ɪtʃ] 動 發癢

A mosquito bite makes you *itch*.
蚊子叮過的地方會發癢。

# J j

**jacket** ['dʒækɪt] 名 夾克，短上衣
This is Kate's new *jacket*.
這是凱特的新夾克。

**jam** [dʒæm] 名 果醬
The boy would like some *jam*.
那個男孩想要些果醬。

**January** [ˈdʒænjuˌɛrɪ, ˈdʒænjuərɪ] 一月
*January* is the first month of the year.
一月是一年中的第一個月。

**Japan** [dʒəˈpæn] 名 日本
She comes from *Japan*.
她是日本人。

**Japanese** [ˌdʒæpəˈniz] 名 日語, 日本人
She teaches *Japanese*.
她教日語。

形 日本人的，日語的
She has many *Japanese* books.
她有許多日語書。

**jar** [dʒɑr] 名 一罐所裝的量(或物)
What a big *jar* of biscuits!
多麼大的一個餅乾筒呀！

**jaw** [dʒɔ] 名 顎，下巴
We move our *jaws* when we eat and talk.
當我們吃飯和說話時會使雙顎產生運動。

**jean** [dʒin,dʒen] 名 牛仔褲
Jack wears a pair of blue *jeans*.
傑克穿了一條藍牛仔褲。

J

**jeep** [dʒip] 名 吉普車
The *jeep* is green.
那輛吉普車是綠色的。

**jelly** ['dʒɛlɪ] 名 果凍
Most children like eating *jelly*.
大多數的孩子喜歡吃果凍。

**jewel** ['dʒuəl,'dʒɪuəl] 名 珠寶，寶石
The rich man has a box of *jewels*.
那個富翁有一箱珠寶。

**jingle** ['dʒɪŋgļ] 動 叮噹響
The bells on the dog's neck *jingle* when it moves.
狗走動時，脖子上的鈴鐺便會叮叮噹噹響。

**job** [dʒɑb] 名 工作
He got a *job* as a clerk.
他得到了一份辦事員的工作。

**jog** [dʒɑg] 動 慢跑
The old man *jogs* every morning.
那個老人每天早上都跑步。

**join** [dʒɔɪn] 動 加入
May I *join* you?
我可以和你們在一起嗎?

**joke** [dʒok] 名 笑話
Sandy is telling a *joke*.
桑迪正在講笑話。

103

**journey** ['dʒɜnɪ] 名 旅行，旅程
They'll make a *journey* to the east of America.
他們將到美國的東部旅行。

**joy** [dʒɔɪ] 名 高興，歡樂
They sing and dance with *joy*.
他們高興得載歌載舞。

**jug** [dʒʌg] 名 (帶柄的)杯，壺
Each of her hands holds a *jug* of water.
她每隻手裏都拿著一杯水。

**juggle** ['dʒʌgl] 動 玩雜耍
The man can *juggle* with six plates.
那個人能耍 6 個盤子。

**juice** [dʒus,dʒɪus] 名 汁
Tom wants two glasses of orange *juice*.
湯姆想要兩杯橘子汁。

**July** [dʒu'laɪ,dʒɪu'laɪ] 名 七月
It's very hot in *July*.
七月裏天氣很熱。

**jump** [dʒʌmp] 動 跳
Who can *jump* over the fence?
誰能跳過那道籬笆？
Let's *jump* rope.
咱們來跳繩吧。

**June** [dʒun,dʒɪun] 名 六月
The first of *June* is National
Children's Day.
6月1日是國際兒童節。

**jungle** ['dʒʌŋgl] 名 叢林，密林
There are many animals in the *jungle*.
那片叢林裏有許多動物。

**just** [dʒʌst] 形 公正的，正直的

Be *just* to Billy.

對比利公正一點。

副 ①正好　②僅僅，只不過

① That's *just* what I want.

　那正是我想要的。

② I *just* wanted to help her.

　我當時只想幫她一下。

**J**

**keep**

**keep** [kip] 動 ①保存 ②保持

① Helen *kept* it for a week.
海倫把它保存了一個星期。

② *Keep* our classroom clean, please!
請保持我們的教室衛生。

**kettle** ['kɛtl] 名 壺

I boil water in a *kettle*.
我用壺燒開水。

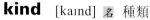

**key** [ki] 名 鑰匙

This is the *key* to the door.
這是那扇門的鑰匙。

**kick** [kɪk] 動 踢

Sandy is *kicking* the ball to Billy.
桑迪正把球踢給比利。

**kid** [kɪd] 名 小孩

How many *kids* do you have?
你有幾個小孩?

**kill** [kɪl] 動 殺死,弄死

That cat *killed* a bird.
那隻貓弄死了一隻鳥。

**kind** [kaɪnd] 名 種類

What *kind* of book do you like best?
你最喜歡哪一類書?

## kindergarten ['kɪndə‚gɑrtn] 名 幼稚園
The children learn to play and work together in *kindergarten*.
孩子們在幼稚園裏學會一起遊戲和相處。

## king [kɪŋ] 名 國王
A *king* lives in a palace.
國王居住在王宮裏。

## kiss [kɪs] 動 吻
Kate *kisses* her mother when she goes to bed.
凱特總要親吻一下媽媽才去睡覺。

## kitchen ['kɪtʃɪn,'kɪtʃən] 名 廚房
Diana always keeps the *kitchen* clean.
戴安娜總是保持廚房衛生。

## kite [kaɪt] 名 風箏
Let's fly a *kite*.
讓我們來放風箏吧。

### kitten ['kɪtn] 名 小貓
The *kitten* is playing.
那隻小貓在玩耍。

### knee [ni] 名 膝蓋
We bend both *knees* when we jump.
我們跳躍時雙膝彎曲。

## knife [naɪf] 名 小刀
I cut the apple with a *knife*.
我用小刀切開蘋果。

### knit [nɪt] 動 編織
Grandmother is *knitting* a scarf.
奶奶在織一條圍巾。

### knock [nɑk] 動 敲
The mailman is *knocking* on the door.
郵差在敲門。

## knot [nɑt] 名 繩結

Can you tie a *knot*?

你會打繩結嗎?

## know [no] 名 ①認識 ②知道，了解

① I *knew* him in high school.

我上中學時認識了他。

② Now I *know* him very well.

現在我很了解他。

## Korea [koˈriə,kɔriə] 名 韓國

*Korea* lies to the east of China.

韓國位於中國的東方。

## Korean [koˈriən,kɔriən] 名 韓國人(的)

Is she a Korean?

她是韓國人嗎?

K

**ladder** ['lædɚ] 名 梯子
They are climbing the *ladder*.
他們正在爬梯子。

**ladle** ['ledl] 名 勺子
Jane moves the soup with a *ladle*.
珍用勺子攪湯。

**lady** ['ledɪ] 名 夫人，女士
Let's go and ask the *lady*.
我們去問問那位女士。

**lake** [lek] 名 湖
There's a boat on the *lake*.
湖面上有一艘小船。

**lamb** [læm] 名 羔羊，小羊
The *lamb* is eating the grass.
那隻羔羊正在吃草。

**lamp** [læmp] 名 燈
Please turn off the *lamp*.
請關燈。

## land [lænd] 名 土地，陸地

Some animals live in the *land* and some live in the sea.

有些動物生活在陸地上，有些動物生活在海洋裏。

動 著陸

The airplane is *landing* at the airport.

那架飛機正在機場降落。

## language ['læŋgwɪdʒ] 名 語言

Is English a difficult *language* to learn?

英語是一門難學的語言嗎？

## large [lɑrdʒ] 形 大的

That's a very *large* shoe.

那是一隻非常大的鞋。

反 small 小的

## last [læst] 形 ①最後的，最末的 ②過去的

① Who was the *last* in the race

在比賽中，誰跑在最後？

② I wrote a letter to him *last* week.

上一星期我寫了一封信給他。

## late [let] 形 遲到的

They are *late* for school.

他們上學遲到了。

## laugh [læf] 動 笑

The boy is *laughing*.

那個男孩正在大笑。

反 cry 哭

## lay [le] 動 ①放置 ②生蛋 ③ lie 的過去式

① Mike *laid* his schoolbag on his desk.

邁克把他的書包放在書桌上。

② Hens *lay* eggs.

母雞下蛋。

**lazy** ['lezɪ] 形 懶惰

The cat is *lazy*.

那隻貓很懶。

**lead** [lid] 動 帶路

Who is going to *lead* the way?

誰為我們帶路?

**leader** ['lidɚ] 名 領導，首領

She is the *leader* of Class 3.

她是三班的班長。

**leaf** [lif] 名 葉子

Most *leaves* are green in the summer.

大多數葉子在夏天是綠色的。

**leak** [lik] 動 滲，漏

The water has *leaked* out.

水已經漏出來了。

**lean** [lin] 動 倚，靠

The boy *leaned* against the wall.

那個男孩倚靠著牆。

　　形 精瘦的

I only eat *lean* meat.

我只吃瘦肉。

　　反 fat 肥的，胖的

**learn** [lɜn] 動 學習

Pupils *learn* a lot of things in school.

學生們在學校裏學到許多東西。

　　同 study 學習

**leather** ['lɛðɚ] 名 皮革

My shoes are made of *leather*.

我的鞋子是皮革製成的。

**leave** [liv] 動 ①離開 ②留下，剩下

① Peter is *leaving* the classroom.
彼得將要離開教室。

② He *left* his books on the desk.
他把書本留在課桌上。

**left** [lɛft] 形 左邊的
Turn to the *left*.
向左轉（拐）
反 right 右邊的

**leg** [lɛg] 名 腿
An ant has six *legs*.
一隻螞蟻有六條腿。

**lemonade** [ˌlɛməˈned] 名 檸檬汁
Jack likes *lemonade* very much.
傑克非常喜歡喝檸檬汁。

**length** [lɛŋ(k)θ] 名 長度
What's the *length* of your ruler?
你的尺有多長？

**lend** [lɛnd] 動 借（出）
Will you *lend* me your bicycle?
你能借我用一下你的腳踏車嗎？

**lesson** [ˈlɛsn] 名 ①（課本中的）一課 ②課程

① This book has 20 *lessons*.
這本書有二十課。

② Sandy takes piano *lessons* from Miss Williams.
桑迪跟威廉斯小姐學彈鋼琴。

**let** [lɛt] 動 讓
The teacher *let* Tom play his guitar.
老師讓湯姆彈吉他。
Let's = Let us 讓我們

**L**

**letter** [ˈlɛtɚ] 名 ①字母 ②信

① Z is the last *letter* in the English alphabet.
Z 是英語字母表中最後一個字母。

② Rose is writing a *letter* to her friend.
羅絲正在給朋友寫信。

**lick** [lɪk] 動 舔
Lucy is *licking* the ice cream.
露西正在舔冰淇淋。

**library** [ˈlaɪbrɛrɪ, laɪbrɪ, ˈlaɪbrərɪ] 名 圖書館
You can borrow books from the *library*.
你可以從圖書館借書。

**lie** [laɪ] 名 謊言
Don't tell me a *lie*.
不要對我說謊。

動 說謊
Did Tom *lie*?
湯姆說謊了嗎?

動 躺
The bear is *lying* on its back.
那隻熊正仰面躺著。

**life** [laɪf] 名 ①生命 ②生活

① I hope you live a long *life*.
我希望你長壽。

② My school *life* is very interesting.
我的學校生活非常有趣。

**lift** [lɪft] 名 電梯
We go up and down the building in a *lift*.
我們乘電梯上下這座樓。

動 舉起
Billy *lifted* the basket up.
比利把籃子舉了起來。

同 raise 舉起

**light** [laɪt] 名 ①光 ②燈

① The sun gives off *light* and heat.
太陽散發出光和熱。

② Please turn on the *light*.
請打開燈。

There are four *lights* in our classroom
我們教室裏有四盞燈。

動 點燃
They are *lighting* a fire. 他們正在點火。

形 輕的
The case is *light*.
那隻箱子很輕。

**lightning** [ˈlaɪtnɪŋ] 名 閃電
Are you afraid of *lightning*?
你害怕閃電嗎?

**like** [laɪk] 動 喜歡
What do you *like* best?
你最喜歡什麼?
反 dislike 不喜歡

介 像、和……一樣
Betty's dress is *like* Jane's.
貝蒂的洋裝和珍的一樣。

**line** [laɪn] 名 ①線 ②排隊
① The fishing *line* is broken.
釣魚線斷了。
② Stand in a *line*.
站成一行。

**lion** [laɪən] 名 獅子
The *lion* is the king of all the animals.
獅子是百獸之王。

**list** [lɪst] 名 名單、目錄
There's a name *list* on the teacher's desk.
講桌上有一張名單。

**listen** ['lɪsṇ] 動 聽

Listen to the tape carefully.
仔細聽錄音。

注

listen, hear 都表示聽，但 listen 表示"注意聽""仔細聽";

hear 表示"聽到，聽見"。

**little** ['lɪtḷ] 形 ①小的 ②幾乎没有，少許的

① The little bird is learning to fly.
那隻小鳥在學飛。

② There's very little butter left.
没有多少奶油了。

比較

little 表示否定語氣"幾乎没有"。 a little 表示肯定語氣"有一些。"

**live** [lɪv] 動 居住，生活

Where do you live?
你住在哪裏?

**living room** ['lɪvɪŋ'rʊm] 名 起居室

Is your living room big?
你們家的客廳大嗎?

**loaf** [lof] 名 麵包

I'll cut the loaf into slices.
我將把一條麵包切成片。

**lock** [lɑk] 名 鎖

Put the lock on the box.
用這把鎖鎖上那個盒子。

**locker** ['lɑkɚ] 名 櫥櫃

There's a shoe in the locker.
櫥櫃裏有一隻鞋。

**lollipop** ['lɑlɪ‚pɑp] 名 棒棒糖

Billy's licking a lollipop.
比利吃棒棒糖。

**long**

**L**

**long** [lɔŋ] 形 長的

The girl's hair is so *long*.

那女孩的頭髮很長。

反 short 短的

**look** [lʊk] 動 看

*Look* at your book.

看你的書。

look for 尋找; look after 照顧;

look up 查(字典、參考書)

**loose** [lus] 形 鬆散的

My tooth is *loose*. I must go to see the dentist.

我的牙齒有些鬆動，我得去看牙醫。

反 tight 緊的

**lose** [luz] 動 丟失

Dick often *loses* his pencil.

迪克經常弄丟鉛筆。

反 find 找到

同 miss 丟掉

**lot** [lɑt] 形 許多

There is a *lot* of honey.

有許多蜂蜜。

There are a *lot* of apples in the basket.

籃子裏有許多蘋果。

a lot of = lots of

**loud** [laʊd] 形 (聲音)大的，響亮的

The music is too *loud*.

音樂聲太大了。

反 low 低聲的，小聲的

**love** [lʌv] 動 愛

Everyone *loves* his parents.

每個人都愛自己的父母。

反 hate 恨

**lovely** ['lʌvlɪ] 形 可愛的
What a *lovely* weather!
多好的天氣啊!

**low** [lo] 形 ①低的 ②矮的
① Jane speaks in a *low* voice.
珍說話聲音很小。
② She sits on a *low* chair.
她坐在一把矮凳上。
反 high 高的

**luck** [lʌk] 名 幸運
You can have good luck and bad *luck*.
你可能有好運, 也可能有惡運。

**lucky** ['lʌkɪ] 形 幸運的
You are *lucky* because you won the first prize.
因爲你得了頭獎, 所以你是幸運的。
反 unlucky 不幸的

**lump** [lʌmp] 形 塊, 塊狀物
Sandy put a *lump* of sugar in his milk.
桑迪在他的牛奶裏放了一塊糖。

**lunch** [lʌntʃ] 名 午飯, 午餐
Mike is having *lunch* with his aunt.
邁克正在和他的姑姑一起吃午餐。

L

**machine** [mə'ʃin] 名 機器

*Machine*s can do many things for us.
機器能幫助我們做許多事情。

**mad** [mæd] 形 ①瘋狂的 ②憤怒的

①Don't go near the *mad* dog.
不要接近那條瘋狗。

②Tom became *mad* when he couldn't find his pen.
湯姆找不到他的鋼筆時，很生氣。

**madam** ['mædəm] 名 女士，夫人

Can I help you, *madam*?
我能為你效勞嗎，夫人？

**magazine** [,mægə'zin] 名 雜誌

They are reading the *magazine*.
他們正在看雜誌。

**magic** ['mædʒɪk] 名 魔術，戲法

**magician** [mə'dʒɪʃən] 名 魔術師

The magician can do many magic tricks.
那個魔術師能夠變出許多種魔術。

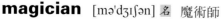

### magnet ['mægnɪt] 名 磁鐵
Mike is playing with a *magnet*.
邁克正在玩一塊磁鐵。

### mail [mel] 名 信件，郵件
There isn't much *mail* today.
今天没有多少郵件。
mailbox 郵箱
air mails 航空郵遞

**M**

## make [mek] 動 做，造
Can you make a kite for me?
你能為我做一個風箏嗎？
maker 製造者

## makeup ['mek,ʌp] 名 化妝

## man [mæn] 名 ①人，人類 ②男人
① *Man* has invented many wonderful things.
人類已經發明了許多美妙的東西。
② Sandy will be a *man* when he grows up.
桑迪長大後會成為一個男子漢。
反 woman 女人
複數 men

### manager ['mænɪdʒɚ] 名 經理
Who wants to be a *manager* ?
誰想成為經理？

### manner ['mænɚ] 名 禮貌
It's a good *manner* to respect others.
尊重別人是有禮貌的行為。

## many ['mɛnɪ] 形 許多的
There aren't *many* beans in the basket.
籃子裏没有太多的豆子了。
反 few 少數的

## map [mæp] 名 地圖

Helen is good at reading *maps*.
海倫善於看地圖。

## March [mɑrtʃ] 名 三月

*March* comes at the end of the winter.
三月了，冬季即將結束。

## mark [mɑrk] 名 分數

Peter got top *marks* on the English test.
彼得在英語考試中得了滿分。

動 批分數，評成績

The teacher is *marking* the exam papers.
那個老師正在批改試卷。

## market ['mɑrkɪt] 名 市場

Billy's father sells fish in the *market*.
比利的父親在市場上賣魚。

supermarket 超級市場

## marry ['mærɪ] 動 結婚

She *married* a soldier.
她和一位士兵結婚。

## mask [mæsk] 名 面具

Mike wears a *mask* on his face.
邁克戴着一個面具。

## match [mætʃ] 名 ①比賽 ②火柴

① Billy's watching the football *match*.
比利正在觀看足球比賽。

② Don't play with *matches*.
不要玩火柴。

## mathematics [,mæθə'mætɪks] 名 數學

Betty doesn't like *mathematics*.貝蒂不喜歡數學。

縮 math

小學課程

Chinese 語文; math 數學; English 英語; history 歷史;

geography 地理; science 自然; drawing 圖畫; fine art 美術;

music 音樂; physical education 體育; computer 電腦

M

**matter** ['mætɚ] 名 事情，問題

What's the *matter*?

發生了什麼事？

**May** [me] 名 五月

May is the fifth month of the year.

五月是一年裏的第五個月。

**may** [me] 助動 可以，可能

*May* I borrow your dictionary?

我可以借用一下你的字典嗎？

The coat *may* be Peter's.

那件大衣可能是彼得的。

**maybe** ['mebɪ,'mebi] 副 也許，可能

*Maybe* I can go, but I'm not sure.

我也許能去，但是我不確定。

同　perhaps 也許，可能

**mayor** ['meɚ, mɛr] 名 市長

As a *mayor*, he is strict with himself.

作為一名市長，他嚴格要求自己。

**meadow** ['mɛdo,'mɛdə] 名 草地，草坪

Grass and flowers grow in a *meadow*.

草地上生長著花草。

**meal** [mil] 名 餐，飯

We have three *meals* a day: breakfast, lunch and supper.

我們一天吃三餐飯：早餐、午餐和晚餐。

**mean** [min] 動 表示……的意思

N *means* north on the map.

"N" 在地圖上表示 "北方"。

**meaning** ['minɪŋ] 名 意思，意義

What's the *meaning* of the word?

這個單字的意思是什麼？

**meat** [mit] 名 肉

We have no *meat*.

我們沒有肉了。

食用肉類

pork 豬肉；  beef 牛肉；  mutton 羊肉；chicken 雞肉；  fish 魚肉

**medicine** ['mɛdəsn] 名 藥

The doctor gave him some *medicine* for his headache.

醫生給了他一些治頭痛的藥。

**meet** [mit] 動 遇見

I'm glad to meet you.

很高興見到你。

**melon** ['mɛlən] 名 瓜

Cucumber is one kind of *melon*.

胡瓜是瓜的一種。

**melt** [mɛlt] 動 熔化，融化

Ice begins to *melt* when you put it in a warm room.

當你把冰放進一個溫暖的房間時，它便開始融化。

**member** ['mɛmbɚ] 名 成員

She is a *member* of our group.

她是我們小組的成員。

**memory** ['mɛmərɪ] 名 記憶力

Their English teacher has a very good *memory*.

他們的英語老師有著非常好的記憶力。

**mend** [mɛnd] 動 修理，修補

Peter can *mend* the broken kite.

彼得會修理那個壞了的風箏。

同  repair 修理

**menu** ['mɛn(j)u,'mɛn(j)u] 名 菜單
Please show me the *menu*.
請給我看一下菜單。

**merry** ['mɛrɪ] 形 快樂的，高興的
*Merry* Christmas! 聖誕快樂!
merry-go-round 旋轉木馬

**M**

**message** ['mɛsɪdʒ] 名 消息、口信
Dad is out. Can I leave a *message* ?
爸爸不在家，我可以留個話嗎?

**metal** ['mɛtl] 名 金屬
Iron, silver and gold are types of *metal*.
鐵、銀和銅是不同類型的金屬。

**meter** ['mitɚ] 名 米，公尺
The line is two *meters* long.
這條繩子兩公尺長。

**midday** ['mɪd,de] 名 正午，中午
He will arrive at *midday*.
他將在中午到達。

**middle** ['mɪdl̩] 形 中間的，中部的
Don't play in the *middle* of the street.
不要在街道中間玩耍。
The tall boy is a *middle* school student.
那位高個子的男孩是中學生。

**midnight** ['mɪd'naɪt] 名 午夜，晚上十二點鐘
Jack often listens to the radio at *midnight*.
傑克經常在午夜聽收音機。

**milk** [mɪlk] 名 牛奶
*Milk* is good for our body.
牛奶對我們身體很好。
milkman 賣或送牛奶的人
milk white 乳白色

## million ['mɪljən] 數 一百萬

The box of jewels cost one *million* dollars.
那箱珠寶價值一百萬美元。
millionaire 百萬富翁

## mind [maɪnd] 名 頭腦，心智

One's *mind* tells him what to do.
一個人的心智教他做事。

動 介意，在乎

Never *mind*!
別介意!

## minute ['mɪnɪt] 名 分鐘

There are sixty *minutes* in an hour.
一小時有 60 分鐘。

## mirror ['mɪrɚ] 名 鏡子

Alice is looking at herself in the *mirror*.
艾麗斯正在照鏡子。

## miss [mɪs] 名 小姐 （用於姓名姓之前大寫；不用於姓名前小寫。）

*Miss* Williams is a good teacher.
威廉斯小姐是個好老師。
Good morning, *miss*!
小姐，早安！

動 ①想念 ②錯過

① I *miss* my parents.
我想念我的父母。
② Helen dreamed she *missed* the train.
海倫夢見她錯過了火車。

## mistake [mə'stek] 名 錯誤

Be careful, don't make another *mistake*.
小心點，別再犯錯了。

## mix [mɪks] 動 混合

First *mix* flour, sugar and water together.
首先，把麵粉、糖和水混和起來。

**modern** ['mɑdɚn] 形 現代的

In *modern* life, computers are used in all kinds of fields.

在現代生活中，電腦被應用於各個領域。

**moment** ['momənt] 名 瞬間

Wait for a *moment*!

稍等一會!

**Monday** ['mʌndɪ] 名 星期一

*Monday* is the second day of a week.

星期一是一周的第二天。

**money** ['mʌnɪ] 名 錢

I have no *money* in my pocket.

我口袋裏沒有錢。

**monkey** ['mʌŋkɪ] 名 猴子

*Monkey* is a kind of funny animal.

猴子是一種很滑稽的動物。

**monster** ['mɑnstɚ] 名 怪物，巨獸

Can you tell a story about a *monster*?

你能說一個關於怪物的故事嗎?

**month** [mʌnθ] 名 月

How many *months* are there in a year? Twelve.

一年裏有多少個月? 12個。

**moon** [mun] 名 月亮

The *moon* is shining as bright as the sun.

月光照得如同陽光一樣明亮。

moon cake 月餅

**mop** [mɑp] 名 拖把

The two pupils used *mops* to clean the floor.

那兩個學生用拖把拖乾淨地板。

## more [mor,mɔr] 形 更多的

That's enough. I don't want any *more*.
那夠了，我不想要更多了。

反 less 較少的

## morning ['mɔrnɪŋ] 名 早晨，上午

It's *morning* when the sun rises.
太陽升起的時候是早晨。

## most [most] 名 大部分

*Most* of the teachers in this school are young.
這所學校的大多數老師是年輕人。

形 (many, much 的最高級) 最……

Tom made the *most* mistakes in the class.
湯姆犯的錯誤在全班同學中是最多的。

## mother ['mʌðɚ] 名 母親

How is your *mother*?
你母親身體好嗎？

## motherland ['mʌðɚ,lænd] 名 祖國

We work hard for our *motherland*.
我們為祖國努力工作。

## motorcycle ['motɚ,saɪkḷ] 名 摩托車

Young men like driving *motorcycles*.
年輕人喜歡騎摩托車。

## mountain ['maʊntṇ,'maʊntɪn] 名 山，大山

Some *mountains* have snow on top.
有些山頂上覆蓋著積雪。

## mouth [maʊθ] 名 嘴

"Keep your *mouth* shut." Mike
said angrily.
"閉嘴，"邁克生氣地說。

**M**

**ove** [muv] 動 搬動，移動
David is helping him *move* the table.
大衛正在幫他搬桌子。

**movie** [muvi] 名 電影
Let's go and see a *movie*.
我們去看場電影吧。

**now** [mo] 動 割
Mr. White is *mowing* his lawn.
懷特先生正在修剪家裏的草坪。

**Mr.** ['mɪstɚ] 名 先生
This is *Mr.* Black.
這是布萊克先生。

**Mrs.** ['mɪsɪz,'mɪsɪs] 名 夫人，太太
This is *Mrs.* Zhang.
這是張太太。

**much** [mʌtʃ] 形 許多的
There isn't *much* honey.
沒有很多蜂蜜了。
How *much* is it?
多少錢？

比較

many 修飾可數名詞，指數目很多；much 修飾不可數名詞，指量
大、程度深。a lot of 既可修飾可數名詞，也可修飾不可數名詞，
既可指數目，又可指量。a lot 單獨使用，不接名詞。

**mud** [mʌd] 名 泥巴

**muddy** ['mʌdɪ] 形 沾滿泥巴的，泥濘的
He has been walking in the mud.
His shoes are *muddy* now.
他一直在泥地裏走。現在，他的的鞋子
滿是泥巴。

**mug** [mʌg] 名 馬克杯
The headmaster is holding a *mug* of tea.
校長正端著一大杯茶。

**mum** [mʌm] 名 媽媽
*Mum*, look at my big balloon.
媽媽，看我的大氣球。
mom（美國口語）媽
mummy（英國兒語）媽

**muscle** ['mʌsḷ] 名 肌肉
Jim exercises his arm *muscles*.
吉姆鍛鍊他的臂膀肌肉。

**museum** [mju'ziəm, mɪu'ziəm, mɪu'zɪəm] 名 博物館
I went to the *museum* by bus.
我乘公車去了博物館。

**music** ['mjuzɪk, 'mɪuzɪk] 名 音樂，樂曲
We have a *music* lesson this afternoon.
今天下午，我們有一節音樂課。

**must** [mʌst] 情態動詞 一定，必須
You *must* finish your homework.
你必須完成你的家庭作業。
You *mustn't* be late.
你一定不能遲到。

**mutton** ['mʌtn̩] 名 羊肉
Diana is cutting the *mutton*.
戴安娜正在切羊肉。

**N**

**nail** [nel] 名 ①指甲　②釘子

　　① Mother is trimming Lucy's *nails* carefully.
　　媽媽小心地爲露茜剪指甲。

　　② Mike hit the *nail* into the wood.
　　邁克把釘子釘進了木板。

**name** [nem] 名 名字
　　What's her *name*? Her *name* is Jane.
　　她叫什麼名字？—珍。

**nap** [næp] 名 小睡，打瞌睡
　　Sue takes a *nap* after her lunch.
　　蘇午飯後睡個覺。

**napkin** ['næpkɪn] 名 餐巾

We use *napkins* to clean our mouths and fingers.
我們用餐巾擦嘴和手指。

**narrow** ['næro,'nærə] 形 狹窄的

Our teacher lives in this *narrow* street.
我們的老師住在這條狹窄的街道上。

　　反　wide 寬闊的

## nasty ['næstɪ] 形 令人討厭的，令人作嘔的

The food has a *nasty* taste.

這種食物味道不好。

## nation ['neʃən] 名 國家

Do you know about some western *nations*?

你了解一些西方國家嗎?

## nationality [,næʃən'ælətɪ] 名 國籍

What *nationality* are you?

你是哪國人?

I'm American.

我是美國人。

## naughty ['nɔtɪ] 形 淘氣的，頑皮的

The *naughty* boy is drawing on the wall.

那個淘氣男孩正在牆上亂畫。

## navy ['nevɪ] 名 海軍

Mike's uncle is in the *navy*.

邁克的叔叔正在海軍服役。

## near [nɪr] 介 在……旁邊，附近

Don't sit *near* the door.

不要坐在門旁邊。

### nearly ['nɪrlɪ] 副 幾乎

The jar is *nearly* empty.

那個瓶子幾乎空了。

### neat [nit] 形 整潔的，整齊的

Sandy keeps his clothes *neat*.

桑迪總保持衣著整潔。

## neck [nɛk] 名 脖子

One's *neck* joins his head and body.

一個人的脖子連接著頭和身體。

necktie 領帶

necklace 項鏈

### need [nid] 动 需要

He *needs* a pair of new shoes.
他需要一雙新鞋。

### needle ['nidḷ] 名 針

We sew with a *needle* and thread.
我們用針線縫衣服。

### neighbor ['nebɚ] 名 鄰居

Our *neighbors* are friendly to us.
我們的鄰居和我們友好相處。

### neither ['niðɚ] 代 兩者都不

I choose *neither* of them.
我不選他們兩個中任何一個。

### neither...nor... 既不……也不……

He *neither* knows *nor* cares what happened.
他既不知道也不關心發生什麼事情。

### nephew ['nɛfju,'nɛfɪu] 名 侄子，外甥

I'm my uncle's *nephew*.
我是我叔叔的侄子。
（我是我舅舅的外甥。）

### nest [nɛst] 名 鳥窩

The *nest* is made from branches, mud and leaves.
那個鳥窩是用樹枝、泥巴和樹葉壘成的。

### net [nɛt] 名 網子

Some boys use *nets* to catch butterflies.
一些男孩用網子捉蝴蝶。

### never ['nɛvɚ] 副 從不，永不

*Never* do this again.
別再這樣做。

131

**new**  [nju,n(I)u] 形 新的

Children like wearing *new* clothes at Christmas.

過聖誕節時，孩子們喜歡穿新衣。

New Year　新年

New Year's Day　元旦

**news**  [njuz,n(I)uz] 名 新聞

I watch the *news* on TV.

我看電視新聞。

**newspaper**  ['njuz,pepɚ] 名 報紙

Father reads the *newspaper* after breakfast

爸爸早飯後看過那份報紙。

**next**  [nɛkst] 形 下一個，其次的

My birthday is *next* Monday.

我的生日是下周一。

**next to** 緊鄰

Mary stands *next to* Sue.

瑪麗緊挨著蘇站著。

**nice**  [naɪs] 形 好的，愉快的

It's a *nice* picture.

那是一幅好畫。

*Nice* to see you.

很高興見到你。

**niece**  [nis] 名 侄女，外甥女

She bought her *niece* a doll last Sunday.

上星期天她給外甥女買了一個布娃娃。

**night**  [naɪt] 名 夜晚

Don't go out at *night*.　晚上不要外出。

反　day 白天

**nine**  [naɪn] 數 九

*Nine* comes after eight.

九在八後面。

**nineteen** [naɪn'tin,naɪn'tin] 數 十九

Her older brother is *nineteen*.

她的大哥十九歲了。

**ninety** ['naɪntɪ] 數 九十

Jim has collected *ninety* coins.

吉姆已經搜集了九十枚硬幣。

**nippy** ['nɪpɪ] 形 寒冷的，刺骨的

It's *nippy* this morning.

今天早上特別冷。

**no** [no] 形 沒有

I have *no* time to wait.

我沒有時間再等了。

Are you hungry, Sandy? — No, I'm not.

桑迪，你餓了嗎? —不，我不餓。

反 yes 是，是的

**nobody** ['no,bɑdɪ,'no,bʌdɪ,'nobədɪ] 代 沒有人

*Nobody* is here.

這兒沒有人。

**nod** [nɑd] 動 點頭

The teacher *nodded* in agreement.

老師點頭同意了。

**noise** [nɔɪz] 名 噪音

Don't make any *noise*, children.

孩子們，別發出聲音。

**none** [nʌn] 名 一個人(物)也沒有

*None* of them came back.

他們中沒有一個人回來。

比較

none 與 no one: none 即可指人，也可指物，表示沒有任何人或東西; no one 只指人，表示沒有一個人。

### nonsense ['nɑnsɛns] 名 胡說，廢話
Don't talk *nonsense*.
勿再胡言。

### noodles ['nudl̩] 名 麵條
They are eating *noodles*.
他們正在吃麵。

### noon [nun] 名 中午，正午
I'll meet you for lunch at *noon*.
中午我接你吃午飯。

### nor [nɔr,弱 nɚ] 介 也不
It's neither cold *nor* hot now.
現在天氣既不冷也不熱。
He won't go there, *nor* will I.
他不去那兒，我也不去。

### north [nɔrθ] 名 北方
On a map, *north* is on the top.
在地圖上，北方在上面。

northwest 西北;　northeast 東北

### nose [noz] 名 鼻子
He has a long *nose*.
他的鼻子很高。

### not [nɑt] 副 不（用於構成否定句）
I do *not* like you.
我不喜歡你。
You are *not* a good boy.
你不是一個好男孩。
I will *not* come tomorrow.
明天我不來。

語法

not 與 be, have, has, do 等連用時，略寫作 −n't 。如:
isn't, aren't, haven't, hasn't, can't, don't, won't等。

**N**

**note** [not] 名 便條，筆記
There's a *note* on the door.
門上有一張便條。

**notebook** ['not,bʊk] 名 筆記本
Rose is writing in her *notebook*.
羅絲正在筆記本上寫字。

**nothing** ['nʌθɪŋ] 名 沒有東西
There's *nothing* in the glass.
玻璃杯裏什麼也沒有。

**notice** ['notɪs] 動 注意
Sorry, I didn't *notice* you.
對不起，我沒有注意到你。

**November** [no'vɛmbɚ] 名 十一月
Thanksgiving comes in *November*.
感恩節是在十一月。

**now** [naʊ] 副 現在
Read loudly *now*, please.
現在，請大聲朗讀。

**number** ['nʌmbɚ] 名 數字
Count these *numbers*, please.
請數一下這些數字。
語法
在數字之前，number 常略作No.。例如:
No. 2　第二。

**nurse** [nɝs] 名 護士
Who's this young *nurse* ?
這個年輕的護士是誰?

**nut** [nʌt] 名 堅果，乾果
*Nuts* have hard shells.
乾果有硬殼。

135

a hippo 一隻河馬

two clusters of grapes 兩串葡萄

five flowers 五朵花

seven mushrooms 七顆蘑菇

eight butterflies 八隻蝴蝶

three caps 三頂帽子

four apples 四個蘋果

six eggs 六個雞蛋

nine coins 九枚硬幣

ten balls 十個球

**oak** [ok] 名 橡樹

*Oak* is a kind of tree.
橡樹是一種樹。

**oatmeal** ['ot,mil] 名 燕麥粥

David ate *oatmeal* for breakfast.
大衛早餐喝的是燕麥粥。

**oar** [or,ɔr] 名 槳

We use *oars* to row a boat.
我們用槳來划船。

**obey** [ə'be,o'be] 動 服從

Dick *obeyed* his mother and went to bed.
迪克聽媽媽的話去上床睡覺。

**ocean** ['oʃən] 名 海洋

The ship is travelling on the
Pacific *Ocean*.
船正在太平洋上航行。

四大洋表示法

the Pacific Ocean 太平洋;　the Atlantic Ocean 大西洋

the Indian Ocean 印度洋; the Arctic Ocean 北極海（北冰洋）

**o'clock** [ə'klɑk] 名 ……點鐘

They'll start at three *o'clock*.

他們將在三點鐘出發。

**October** [ɑk'tobɚ] 名 十月

*October* Ten is our National Day.

十月十日是國慶日。

**odd** [ɑd] 形 奇數的

One, three, five, seven and nine are *odd* numbers.

一、三、五、七、九都是奇數。

反 even 偶數的

**of** [ɑv,ʌv,弱 əv] 介 ①屬於…… ②關於

① A friend *of* mine works in Taipei.

我的一個朋友在台北工作。

② I've never heard *of* such things.

我從沒有聽說過這樣的事情。

**off** [ɔf] 副 ①離開 ②關掉 ③脫掉

① Get *off* the bus, please.

請下車。

② I'm ready. Turn *off* the lights.

我準備好了，關燈吧。

③ It's too hot, take *off* your coat.

太熱了，脫掉大衣吧。

**offer** ['ɔfɚ,'ɑfɚ] 動 提供，給予

Peter *offered* to help Mary repair her bicycle.

彼得主動幫助瑪麗修腳踏車。

**office** ['ɔfɪs,'ɑfɪs] 名 辦公室

This is our English teacher's *office*.

這是我們英語老師的辦公室。

**officer** ['ɔfəsɚ, 'ɑfəsɚ] 名 軍官

The *officer* is very serious.

這位軍官非常嚴屬。

one o'clock 1 點鐘

two o'clock 2 點鐘

five o'clock 5 點鐘

six o'clock 6 點鐘

nine o'clock 9 點鐘

ten o'clock 10 點鐘

three o'clock 3 點鐘

four o'clock 4 點鐘

seven o'clock 7 點鐘

eight o'clock 8 點鐘

eleven o'clock 11 點鐘

twelve o'clock 12 點鐘

## often ['ɔfən,'ɔftən] 副 經常，常常

We eat rice *often*.
我們經常吃飯。

## oh [o] 嘆 唷，哎呀，啊

*Oh*, dear!
天哪!

*Oh*, how beautiful you are !
啊，太漂亮了!

## oil [ɔɪl] 名 油

We use peanut *oil* for cooking.
我們用花生油炒菜。

David is putting *oil* in his car.
大衛在給汽車加油。

## okay [o'ke,'o'ke] 嘆 好吧(一般縮作OK)

"Will you help me?"
"你幫幫我好嗎?"
"*Ok*, I will."
"好的。"

副 好的，令人滿意的
Sandy did *OK* on this exam.
桑迪這次考試考得不錯。

## old [old] 形 ①舊的 ②年老的 ③年齡的

① It's an *old* hat.
那是一頂舊帽子。

反 new 新的

② The *old* people are as active as the young.
那些老年人和年輕人一樣活躍。

反 young 年輕的

③ How *old* is your grandmother?
你奶奶年紀多大了?
She's seventy years *old*.
她七十歲了。

**on** [ɑn,ɔn] 介 在……上面
What's *on* the grass?
草地上有什麼？

**once** [wʌns] 數 一次
We have a music lesson *once* a week.
我們一周上一節音樂課。

at once 立刻；once more 再一次；once upon a time 從前

**one** [wʌn] 數 一個，單個
I have two books and you have only *one*.
我有兩本書，你只有一本。

比較

a 和 one：a 只表"一"，沒有和其它數詞對比的意思，one 則強調
數目是"一個"，而不是"幾個"。

**onion** ['ʌnjən,'ʌnjɪn] 名 洋蔥
Mary is cutting the *onions*.
瑪麗正在切洋蔥。

**only** ['onlɪ] 副 僅僅，只
He *only* waited a few minutes.
他只等了幾分鐘。

形 唯一的，僅有的
Billy is an *only* son.
比利是個獨生子。

**onto** ['ɑntu,弱 'ɑutu,'ɑntə] 介 在……之上
The child climbed up *onto* his father's back.
那孩子爬到了父親的背上。

**open** ['opən] 動 打開
I *opened* the door to let Mary in.
我打開門讓瑪麗進來。
反 close 關；shut 關

**opposite** ['ɑpəzɪt] 形 相反的，對面的

She stands *opposite* to her teacher.

她站在老師的對面。

名 反義詞

Light is the *opposite* of heavy.

輕是重的反義詞。

**or** [ɔr,弱ɚ] 連 ①或者，還是 ②否則

① Did Sandy want beans *or* ice cream?

桑迪想要豆子還是冰淇淋?

② Eat some beans first *or* you can't have ice cream.

先吃一些豆子，否則你不能吃冰淇淋。

**orange** ['ɔrɪndʒ,'ɑrɪndʒ,'ɑrəndʒ] 名 ①橘子 ②橘子汁

① Mother bought a basket of *oranges*.

媽媽買了一籃橘子。

② I would like some *orange* juice.

我想喝點橘子汁。

orange juice　橘子汁

形 橘黃色的，橙色的

Rose likes the *orange* dress.

羅絲喜歡那條橘黃色的裙子。

**orchard** ['ɔrtʃɚd] 名 果園

This is a small apple *orchard*.

這是個小蘋果園。

**order** ['ɔrdɚ] 動 命令

The doctor *ordered* her to stay in bed.

醫生囑咐她臥床休息。

名 ①命令 ②秩序

① They obey their monitor's *order*.

他們服從班長的命令。

② Keep the class in *order*.

維持班上的紀律。

**organ** ['ɔrgən] 名 風琴

No one can play the *organ* in our class.
我們班上沒有人會彈風琴。

**other** ['ʌðɚ] 形 其餘的（人或物），另外的(人或物)

These two pencils are mine, the *others* are Sue's.
這兩枝鉛筆是我的，其餘的都是蘇的。

**one...the other...** 一個……另一個……

One pencil is blue, the *other* is red.
一枝鉛筆是藍色的，另一枝鉛筆是紅色的。

O

**ouch** [autʃ] 嘆 哎喲

"*Ouch*, my foot."
"哎喲，我的腳。"

**ought** [ɔt] 動 應當，應該

You *ought* to say sorry.
你應該說對不起。

**out** [aut] 副 ①出外，向外 ②不在家

① Let's go *out* for some fresh air.
讓我們出去呼吸新鮮空氣吧。

反 in 在裏邊

② Don't go to Betty's. She's *out*.
別去貝蒂家了，她不在家。

**outdoors** ['aut,dorz] 副 在戶外

The children like to play *outdoors*.
孩子們喜歡在戶外活動。

**outside** ['aut'saɪd] 名 外表

The *outside* of the watermelon is green and dark green.

西瓜的表面是青綠色的。

副 在外面，在外邊
Please wait *outside*. 請在外邊等。

反 inside 在裏邊,在裏面

**oven** ['ʌvən] 名 烤爐，烤箱
Bread is baked in an *oven*.
麵包是在烤箱裏烤的。

**over** ['ovə] 介 在……之上,橫過
Put a cloth *over* the table.
在桌子上鋪一塊桌布。
He holds an umbrella *over* her.
他為她撐著一把傘。
反 under 在……之下
副 結束
Class is *over*. See you later.
下課了。再見。

**owe** [o] 動 欠，負債
Tom *owes* Jim one dollar.
湯姆欠吉姆一塊錢。

**own** [on] 形 自己的，私有的
David has his *own* house.
大衛有自己的房子。

**ox** [ɑks] 名 牛
An *ox* is used for working in the field.
牛用於田間勞動。

**owl** [aʊl] 名 貓頭鷹
An *owl* comes out at night.
貓頭鷹在夜間出來。

**pack** [pæk] 動 收拾

They *pack* their bags to go on vacation.
他們收拾行李準備度假。

**packet** ['pækɪt] 名 小袋，小包，小盒

How many worksheets are there in the
*packet*?
袋子裏有多少張工作單？

**page** [pedʒ] 名 頁

Did we stop at *page* 24 last time?
上次,我們(講)到 24 頁嗎？

**pail** [pel] 名 桶

Jack took a *pail* of water from the well.
傑克從井裏打了一桶水。

**pain** [pen] 名 痛疼，痛苦

Tom has a *pain* in his leg.
湯姆的腿疼。

反 joy 快樂

**paint** [pent] 動 ①油漆 ②畫畫

① *Paint* the door blue, ok?
把門漆成藍色, 好嗎？
② Mary is *painting* a picture.
瑪麗在畫畫。

**pair** [pɛr,pær] 名 一雙，一對

Would you like a *pair* of shoes like this?

你想要一雙這樣的鞋嗎？

in pairs 兩人一組

**P**

**palace** ['pælɪs,'pæləs] 名 宮殿

Who lives in this *palace*?

誰住在這座宮殿裏？

Young Palace 少年宮

**pale** [pel] 形 蒼白的

You look *pale*. You'd better go to bed.

你看起來臉色蒼白，你最好上床休息。

**palm** [pɑm] 名 手掌

Betty says,"Show me your left *palm*."

貝蒂說："把左手掌伸給我看。"

**pan** [pæn] 名 平底鍋，淺鍋

Mother frys eggs in the *pan*.

媽媽用這個平底鍋裏煎鷄蛋。

**pants** ['pænts] 名 褲子

Dick changed into another pair of *pants*.

迪克換了一條褲子。

**paper** ['pepɚ] 名 ①紙 ②試卷，試題

① Take out a piece of *paper*.

拿出一張紙來。

② The geography *paper* is difficult.

地理試題很難。

**parcel** ['pɑrsl̩] 名 包裹

What a big *parcel*!

多麼大的一個包裹啊！

**pardon** ['pɑrdn̩] 名 原諒，寬恕

I beg your *pardon*.

對不起,請再說一遍。(希望對方重覆說過的話。)

### parent ['pɛrənt,'pærənt] 名 父親或母親

Tom came with his *parents*.
湯姆和他父母親一起來的。

### park [pɑrk] 名 公園

Some old people are dancing in the *park*.
一些老人正在公園裏跳舞。

動 停車

Can he *park* his car here?
他可以在這兒停車嗎?

P

## part [pɑrt] 名 部分

Look at the easy *part* first, then the hard *part*.
先看容易的部分，然後再看難的那部分。

反 whole 全部

## partner ['pɑrtnɚ] 名 伙伴，合夥人

Choose a *partner* for us.
爲我們挑選一個伙伴吧。

### party ['pɑrtɪ] 名 聚會，集合

We enjoyed Betty's birthday *party*.
我們在貝蒂的生日聚會上玩得很愉快。
the Party 政黨

## pass [pæs] 動 ①傳遞 ②及格

① *Pass* Jim his exercise book.
把作業本遞給吉姆。
② Study hard or you can't *pass* the final exam.
要努力學習不然你期末考會不及格。

反 fail 不及格

## passage ['pæsɪdʒ] 名 一段

Recite the first two *passages*.
背誦前兩段。

## passenger ['pæsndʒɚ] 名 乘客

Count the *passengers* on the bus.
數一下車上有多少乘客。

## past [pæst] 介 ①經過 ②過了

① Do you walk *past* the shop every day?
你每天經過那個商店嗎?

② I got home at half *past* ten.
我十點半到家。

## patch [pætʃ] 名 補釘

No one wears clothes with *patches*
in our class.
我們班上沒有人穿帶補釘的衣服。

## path [pæθ] 名 小路

The *path* goes through the field.
小路穿過這片田地。

## patient ['peʃənt] 形 耐心的

Be *patient!* Wait a few minutes!
耐心點! 等幾分鐘!

## pattern ['pætɚn] 名 ①式樣,圖樣 ②句型

① Mother makes her dress from the *pattern*.
媽媽按照圖樣剪裁裙子。

② Look at the *patterns* on the
blackboard.
請看黑板上的句型。

## pavement ['pevmənt] 名 人行道

Don't ride your bicycle on the *pavement*.
不要在人行道上騎腳踏車。

## pay [pe] 動 付款

I *paid* two dollars for the dictionary.
我付了兩美元買這本辭典。

**P**

**pea** [pi] 名 豌豆
Green *peas* are good to eat.
青豌豆好吃。

**peace** [pis] 名 和平
Many people hope to live in *peace*.
許多人都希望平平安安過日子。
反 war 戰爭

**peak** [pik] 名 尖端，頂峰
The plane flew over the highest *peak*.
飛機飛過了最高的頂峰。

**pearl** [pɚl] 名 珍珠
Is that a *pearl* necklace?
那是一串珍珠項鏈嗎?

**peasant** ['pɛzn̩t] 名 農民
The life of *peasants* becomes well.
農民的生活變好了。

**peel** [pil] 剝……皮，削皮
Sandy is *peeling* a banana.
桑迪正在剝香蕉皮。
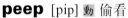
名 皮
Throw the banana *peel* in the garbage.
把香蕉皮扔進垃圾箱。

**peep** [pip] 動 偷看
Don't *peep* at others' letters.
不要偷看別人的信件。

**pen** [pɛn] 名 鋼筆
I write letters with *pen*.
我用鋼筆寫信。

penknife 鉛筆刀; penfriend 筆友

**P**

pencil

**pencil** ['pɛnsḷ] 名 鉛筆

You should write with *pencil*.

你應該用鉛筆寫。

**penny** ['pɛnɪ] 名 便士

Put a *penny* in it then you can use the phone.

往裏投一便士，你就能打電話了。

**people** ['pipḷ] 名 ①人們　②民族

① How many *people* are there in your family?

你家裏有幾個人?

② The Chinese are hardworking and brave *people*.

中華民族是勤勞勇敢的民族。

**perfect** ['pɝfɪkt] 形 極好的，完美的

Nobody is *perfect*.

人無完人。

**perhaps** [pɚ'(h)æps, præps] 副 或許，可能

*Perhaps* I lost the money.

或許我把錢丟了。

**person** ['pɝsn̩] 名 人

He's just the *person* we need.

他正是我們所需要的人。

**pet** [pɛt] 名 寵物

Is that your *pet*?

那是你的寵物嗎?

**phone** [fon] 名 電話

Do you know his *phone* number?

你知道他的電話號碼嗎?

動 打電話

Did anybody *phone* ?

有人來電話嗎?

152

**photograph** ['fotə,græf] 名 照片
Let me take a *photograph* of you.
讓我給你們拍張照吧。

**piano** [pɪˈæno,pɪˈænə,pɪˈɑno] 名 鋼琴
Sue plays the *piano* very well.
蘇鋼琴彈得很好。

**P**

**pick** [pɪk] 動 ①拾，撿 ②採摘
① *Pick* up the pieces of the paper.
撿起一張張紙。
② Don't *pick* flowers!
不要摘花!

**picnic** ['pɪknɪk] 名 野餐
They are having a *picnic*.
他們正在野餐。

**picture** ['pɪktʃɚ] 名 圖片，畫像
Paint a *picture* of yourself.
給你自己畫張像。

**pie** [paɪ] 名 餡餅
Would you like an apple *pie*?
你想要一塊蘋果派嗎?

**piece** [pis] 名 一份，一張，一塊，一支
Tom passed Sandy a *piece* of red chalk.
湯姆遞給桑迪一枝紅粉筆。

**pig** [pɪg] 名 豬
The *pig* is more than two
hundred pounds.
這頭豬超過了 200 磅。

**pillow** ['pɪlo,'pɪlə] 名 枕頭
My *pillow* is orange.
我的枕頭是橘黃色的。

**pin** [pɪn] 名 大頭針

Be careful! Some *pins* are on the floor.

小心! 地板上有大頭針。

**pine** [paɪn] 名 松樹

*Pine* is a kind of evergreen tree.

松樹是一種常青樹。

**pink** [pɪŋk] 形 粉紅色的

Don't you like the *pink* flowers?

難道你不喜歡那些粉紅色的花嗎?

**pioneer** [ˌpaɪə'nɪr] 名 先鋒

They are Young *Pioneers*.

他們是少年隊員。

**pipe** [paɪp] 名 管子

The water *pipe* needs to be repaired.

這個水管需要修理。

**pirate** ['paɪrət,'paɪrɪt] 名 海盜

The *pirate* in the film is very cruel.

電影裏的那個海盜非常冷酷。

**pity** ['pɪtɪ] 名 遺憾, 可惜

What a *pity* that you can't come tonight.

真可惜你今天晚上來不了。

**pizza** ['pitsə] 名 批薩

Did you have *pizza*?

你吃過批薩嗎?

**place** [ples] 名 地方

Where is this *place*?

這個地方在哪兒?

**plan** [plæn] 名 計劃

Have you made your travel *plans*?

你訂好旅行計劃了嗎?

## plant [plænt] 名 植物

No one looks after those wild *plants*.
没有人照管那些野生植物。

## plastic ['plæstɪk] 名 塑膠

Many things are made of *plastic*.
許多東西都是塑膠製成的。

## plate [plet] 名 盤子

There is some food on the *plate*.
盤子裏有一些食物。

## platform ['plæt,fɔrm] 名 講臺

Sandy is standing near the *platform*.
桑迪站在講臺旁邊。

## play [ple] 動 玩

Billy, come and *play* with us.
比利，過來和我們一起玩吧。

名 戲劇，劇本
Has Jane ever been in a *play*?
珍曾經演過戲嗎？

## playground ['ple,graʊnd] 名 操場

The children are playing on the
*playground*.
孩子們正在操場上玩。

## please [pliz] 動 請

Give her the knife and fork, *please*.
請把刀叉給她。
*Please* come in.
請進。

## plenty ['plɛntɪ] 名 大量的，充足的

There are *plenty* of books for us to read in the library.
圖書館裏有大量的書供我們閱讀。

**plough**

**P**

**plough** [plaʊ] 動 犁，耕
The farmer is *ploughing* the field.
那個農夫正在耕地。

**P.M., p.m.** ['pi 'ɛm] 下午，午後
We'll have a meeting at 3 *p.m.*.
我們下午三點鐘開會。

**pocket** ['pɑkɪt] 名 口袋
Look, Billy's *pockets* are full of candy.
看，比利的口袋裏裝滿了糖果。
pocket money 零花錢

**poem** ['po•ɪm,'po•əm] 名 詩
Learn this *poem* by heart.
背誦這首詩。

**poet** ['po•ɪt,'po•ət] 名 詩人
Li Bai is a famous *poet* of the Tang Dynasty.
李白是唐代的一位著名詩人。

**point** [pɔɪnt] 動 指向
It's rude to *point* at others.
用手指人是很不禮貌的。

**poison** ['pɔɪzn] 名 毒藥
Sandy said,"It tastes like *poison*."
桑迪說：「它嘗起來像毒藥一樣。」

**pole** [pol] 名 竿子
A monkey can climb up the *pole* very quickly.
猴子能非常快地爬到竿頂。

**police** [pə'lis] 名 警察
If you want to call the *police*, you dial 119.
如果你想叫警察的話，請打119。

policeman 男警察； policewoman 女警察；

a police station 警察局； police box 警察崗亭

**polish** ['pɑlɪʃ] 動 磨光，拋光
Jim is *polishing* the floor.
吉姆正在擦地板。

**polite** [pə'laɪt] 形 有禮貌的
It's *polite* to say "Thank you"
when somebody helps you.
當別人幫助你的時候，說聲 "謝謝" 是很禮貌的。

**pond** [pɑnd,pɔnd] 名 池塘
There are frogs in that *pond*.
那個池塘裏有青蛙。

**pool** [pul] 名 池子
They swim in the big swimming *pool*.
他們在那個大游泳池裏游泳。

**poor** [pʊr] 形 貧窮的
He came from a *poor* family.
他出生於一個窮人家庭。
反　rich 富有的

**popcorn** ['pɑp,kɔrn] 名 爆玉米花
Mike paid one dollar for the *popcorn*.
邁克花一美元買爆米花。

**popular** ['pɑpjələ] 形 ①受歡迎的　②流行的
① Betty is *popular* among the boys.
貝蒂在男孩中很受歡迎。
② He likes to listen to *popular* music.
他喜歡聽流行音樂。

**pork** [pork,pɔrk] 名 豬肉
*Pork* is six yuan for one jin.
豬肉 6 塊錢一斤。

**post** [post] 動 郵，寄
Dick *posted* a parcel and two letters today.
迪克今天寄了一個包裹和兩封信。
postcard 賀卡；postman 郵遞員；post office 郵局

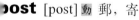

**pot** [pɑt] 名 鍋，壺，罐，盆
The tea in the *pot* is hot.
壺裏的茶是熱的。

**potato** [pə'teto] 名 馬鈴薯
Do you know where *potatoes* grow?
你知道馬鈴薯生長在哪裏嗎？

**pour** [por,pɔr,pʊr] 動 倒、注
She *poured* two cups of coffee.
她倒了兩杯咖啡。

**practise** ['præktɪs] 動 練習
Sue is *practising* on the piano.
蘇在練習鋼琴。

**praise** [prez] 動 表揚、讚揚
The teacher *praised* Mike for his courage.
老師讚揚邁克的勇氣。

名 讚揚
He had a lot *praise* for her work.
他對她的工作大加讚賞。

**pram** [præm] 名 手推嬰兒車
The baby is lying in his *pram*.
那孩子正躺在嬰兒車裏。

**prawn** [prɔn] 名 明蝦
*Prawn* tastes good.
明蝦好吃。

**prepare** [prɪ'pɛr,prɪ'pær] 動 準備
They have no time to *prepare* a meal.
他們沒有時間準備飯。

**present** ['prɛzn̩t] 名 禮物
Here's a *present* for you, Billy.
比利，送給你這個禮物。

## president ['prɛz(ə)dənt] 名 總統

George Washington was the first *president* of America.

喬治・華盛頓是美國第一位總統。

## press [prɛs] 動 按，壓

*Press* the doorbell, Sue.

蘇，按一下門鈴。

**P**

## pretty ['prɪtɪ] 形 漂亮的，可愛的

Jane looks very *pretty* in that hat.

珍戴那頂帽子看起來非常漂亮。

## price [praɪs] 名 價格，價錢

The *price* of his watch is 100 dollars.

他手錶的售價是一百美元。

## prince [prɪns] 名 王子

A *prince* is the son of a king.

王子是國王的兒子。

## princess ['prɪnsɪs] 名 公主

The *princess* will marry Prince Charles today.

那位公主今天將和查爾斯王子結婚。

## prison ['prɪzn̩] 名 監獄

The thief was sent to *prison*.

那個小偷被判入獄。

## prize [praɪz] 名 獎品

Who won the first *prize*?

誰獲得了第一獎？

## professor [prə'fɛsɚ] 名 教授

*Professor* Wang is a kind man.

王教授是一個和藹可親的人。

**159**

**promise** ['prɑmɪs] 名 諾言

    Keep your *promise*, please!

    請遵守諾言。

    I can't *promise*, but I'll do my best.

    我不能承諾，但我會盡最大努力。

**protect** [prə'tɛkt] 動 保護

    You need to *protect* your eyes.

    你需要保護好眼睛。

**proud** [praʊd] 形 自豪的，得意的

    Jim is *proud* of his new model plane.

    吉姆爲他的新飛機模型感到自豪。

**pudding** ['pʊdɪŋ] 名 布丁

    Do you like some *pudding*?

    你喜歡吃布丁嗎?

**pull** [pʊl] 動 拉，扯，拽

    Tom said,"He *pulled* my ear."

    湯姆説:"他拽了我的耳朵。"

    反　push 推

**pump** [pʌmp] 動 打氣，充氣

    He's *pumping* up the bicycle tires.

    他在爲腳踏車充氣。

**pumpkin** ['pʌmpkɪn,'pʌŋkɪn] 名 南瓜

    A *pumpkin* is a kind of vegetable.

    南瓜是一種蔬菜。

**puncture** ['pʌŋktʃɚ] 名 刺孔，刺痕

    There is a *puncture* in the inner tube.

    内胎被扎了一個孔。

**pupil** ['pjupl̩,'pɪupl̩] 名 學生

    All *pupils* are doing morning exercises.

    所有的學生都在做體操。

**puppet** ['pʌpɪt] 名 木偶

Sandy and Sue made a *puppet*.
桑迪和蘇做了一個木偶。

a puppet show 木偶戲

**P**

**push** [pʊʃ] 動 推

You pull, I'll *push*.
你拉，我推。

**put** [pʊt] 動 放

*Put* plates and dishes into the cupboard.
把盤子和碟子放在碗櫥裏。

put·on 穿上；   put down 放下；

put up 舉起．拿起，建造

**pyjamas** (英)
**pajamas** (美)   [pə'dʒæməz] 名 睡衣褲

Professor Boffin wore pajamas to go to
work once.
博芬教授有一次穿着睡衣去上班。

**puzzle** ['pʌzl] 名 謎，謎語

Can you find the answer to the *puzzle?*
你能找到那個謎底嗎？

Jigsaw puzzle 拼圖遊戲；crossword puzzle　填字遊戲

**quarrel**

**quarrel** ['kwɔrəl,kwɑrəl] 動 爭吵，吵架
Don't *quarrel*, children!
別吵了，孩子們!

**quarter** [kwɔrtɚ] 名 一刻鐘，四分之一
Now it's a *quarter* past seven.
現在是七點十五分。
The yellow part is in a *quarter* of the circle.
黃色部分佔圓的四分之一。

**queen** [kwin] 名 女王，王后
Some countries are ruled by *queens*.
世界上有些國家由女王統治。

**question** ['kwɛstʃən] 名 問題
May I ask a *question*, Miss Wu?
吳老師，我可以問你一個問題嗎?
question mark 問號

**queue** [kju,kɪu] 動 排隊
They *queued* for an hour.
他們排了一小時的隊。

**quick** [kwɪk] 形 快的，迅速的

　　Be *quick* or we'll get wet.

　　快一點，否則我們就會被淋濕了。

　　反　slow 慢的

**quickly** ['kwɪklɪ] 副 快地，迅速地

　　Mike did his homework *quickly* and went out to play.

　　邁克快速做完家庭作業，便去玩耍了。

**quiet** ['kwɑɪət] 形 安靜的，輕聲的

　　Sh! Be *quiet*, she is asleep.

　　噓！安靜，她睡著了。

　　反　noisy 嘈雜的

**quite** [kwɑɪt] 副 相當，確實

　　He plays the piano *quite* well.

　　他鋼琴彈得相當好。

**quiz** [kwɪz] 名 測驗，知識競賽

　　Don't worry, it's only a *quiz*.

　　別擔心，這只是一次小測驗。

R

### rabbit ['ræbɪt] 名 兔子

A *rabbit* jumps and runs very fast.
兔子跑跳都很快。

### race [res] 名 比賽

The white horse came in first in the *race*.
那匹白馬在比賽中獲得第一名。

### racket ['rækɪt] 名 網球拍

Hold this *racket*. Let's begin.
拿著這隻球拍，我們開始吧。

### radio ['redɪ‚o] 名 收音機

Turn down the *radio*, please.
請把收音機關小一點。

### railroad ['rel‚rod] 名 (美) 鐵路
### railway ['rel‚we] 名 (英)

A train moves on the *railroad*.
火車在鐵路上奔馳。

### rain [ren] 動 下雨

It's *raining* outside.
外面正在下雨。

### rainbow ['ren‚bo] 名 彩虹

# raincoat ['ren,kot] 名 雨衣

Don't stand in the *rain* without raincoat or you'll get sick.
不要不穿雨衣在雨中站著，否則你會生病的。

表天氣的詞語

cloud 雲；frost 霜；fog 霧；ice 冰；rain 雨；

lightning 閃電；thunder 雷；storm 風暴；snow 雪

**R**

# rainy ['renɪ] 形 下雨的，多雨的

I met her on a *rainy* afternoon.
我在一個雨天的下午碰上了她。

# raise [rez] 動 舉起，抬起

*Raise* your eyes from your book, Dick.
迪克，抬起頭來，別看書。

# rarely ['rɛrlɪ,'ræ>rlɪ] 副 極少地，罕見地

I *rarely* see Sue. 我很少看見蘇。

## rather ['ræðɚ] 副 寧可，寧願

He would *rather* walk than take a bus.
他寧願走路，也不願坐公共汽車。

## raw [rɔ] 形 生的

Sometimes we eat *raw* vegetables.
我們有時吃生蔬菜。

# reach [ritʃ] 動 ①到達　②伸手去取

① They will *reach* Tainan tomorrow morning.
　明天早上他們就到台南了。

比較

reach, arrive in(at), get to: reach 是及物動詞、必須加地點名詞，如
reach Kaohsiung 到達高雄；arrive 是不及物動詞，與 in 一起表示到
達一個大地方，如 arrive in London 到達倫敦，與 at 連用，表示到
達一個小地方，如 arrive at the station 到達車站；get to 後面接名
詞，如果接副詞去掉 to，如 get to Taipei 到達台北，get home 到家

**read**

② Can you *reach* the jam on the cupboard?
你能伸手拿到碗櫥上的果醬嗎？

**read** [rid] 動 讀
Peter has *read* half of the book till now.
到目前為止，彼得已經讀了那本書的一半。

**reader** ['ridɚ] 名 讀者

**reading room** 閱覽室，校對室

**ready** ['rɛdɪ] 形 準備好的
Are you *ready*? 你們準備好了嗎？
*Ready*, steady, go!
各就各位，預備，跑！(賽跑開始時的口令)

**real** ['riəl,ril,'rɪəl] 形 真正的
This ring is not made of *real* gold.
這枚戒指不是由純金做的。

**really** ['riəlɪ,'rilɪ,'rɪəlɪ,'rɪlɪ] 副 真正地
I *really* want to make friends with you.
我真想和你交朋友。

**reason** ['rizn̩] 名 原因，理由
Tell me the *reason* why you were late.
告訴我你遲到的原因。

**receive** [rɪ'siv] 動 接收，收到
Did you *receive* a letter from your sister yesterday?
昨天你收到你妹妹的來信了嗎？

**record** ['rɛkɚd] 名 ①唱片 ②記錄
① Mary keeps all the *records* that she bought.
瑪麗保留著她買來的所有唱片。
② Keep a *record* of all your work.
記錄你所有的工作。

[rɪ'kɔrd] 動 錄音
To *record*, press both buttons.
要錄音，同時按下兩個按鈕。

**recorder** [rɪ'kɔrdɚ] 名 錄音機

**red** [rɛd] 形 紅色的

You must stop at a *red* light.

紅燈亮時，你必須停下來。

**R**

**refrigerator** [rɪ'frɪdʒə,retɚ] 名 冰箱

A *refrigerator* is used to keep food and drinks cold.

冰箱被用於冷藏食物和飲料。

**refuse** [rɪ'fjuz] 動 拒絕

Alice *refused* to go to the movies with us.

艾麗斯拒絕和我們一起去看電影。

**regret** [rɪ'grɛt] 動 懊悔，遺憾

Jim *regrets* that he didn't go to the party.

吉姆後悔他沒有參加聚會。

**remember** [rɪ'mɛmbɚ] 動 記住，記憶

Did you *remember* Peter's birthday, Tom?

湯姆，你記得彼得的生日嗎?

反 forget 忘記

**renew** [rɪ'n(j)u,rɪ'nɪu] 動 續借

Jane went to the library to *renew* the book.

珍去圖書館續借了那本書。

**repair** [rɪ'pɛr,rɪ'pær] 動 修理

Can you *repair* the radio for me?

你能為我修理一下收音機嗎?

**repeat** [rɪ'pit] 動 重覆

Please *repeat* after me, children.

孩子們，請跟著我重覆。

**reply** [rɪ'plaɪ] 動 回答

Tom didn't *reply* to the teacher's questions.

湯姆沒有回答出老師的問題。

**report** [rɪ'port,rɪ'pɔrt] 名 報告

I wrote a *report* about ancient China.
我寫了一篇關於古代中國的報告。

**R**

**rest** [rɛst] 名 ①休息 ②剩餘部分

① Class is over. Let's have a *rest* for
ten minutes.

下課了，我們休息十分鐘吧。

② Where are the *rest* of the students?
剩餘的學生在哪兒？

動 休息

It's time to *rest*. 到休息的時間了。

**restaurant** ['rɛstərənt, 'rɛstə.rɑnt] 名 飯館

They are eating in the *restaurant*.
他們正在飯館裏吃飯。

**result** [rɪ'zʌlt] 名 結果

What's the *result* of your test?
你的考試成績怎麼樣？

**return** [rɪ'tɜn] 動 歸還

We should *return* these books before
the vacation.

我們應該在假期之前歸還這些書。

**ribbon** ['rɪbən] 名 絲帶，緞帶

Betty tied a pink *ribbon* around the present.
貝蒂在禮物上繫了一條粉紅色緞帶。

**rice** [raɪs] 名 ①水稻 ②米飯

① We need a lot of water to grow *rice*.
種水稻需要很多水。

② Billy ate two bowls of *rice*.
比利吃了兩碗米飯。

**rich** [rɪtʃ] 形 富的，富有的

The man is very *rich*, but he lives a simple life.
那個人非常富有，但他卻過著簡樸的生活。

**ride** [raɪd] 動 騎

Can you *ride* a horse?
你會騎馬嗎?

**right** [raɪt] 形 ①正確的 ②右邊的

① Whose answer is *right*?
誰的答案是正確的?

反 wrong 錯誤的

② Dick holds a piece of chalk in his
*right* hand.
迪克右手拿著一枝粉筆。

Turn *right*! 向右轉!

反 left 左邊的

**ring** [rɪŋ] 名 戒指

Mrs. White wears a *ring* on her finger.
懷特夫人手上戴著一枚戒指。

動 (鈴、鐘)響

Don't leave your seats until the bell *ring*s.
鈴響以後你才能離開你的座位。

**rise** [raɪz] 動 升起,上升

What time does the sun *rise*?
太陽什麼時候升起?

反 fall 下降

**river** ['rɪvɚ] 名 河

Many people go fishing at the *river*.
許多人去河邊釣魚。

**road** [rod] 名 道路

The *road* goes to the city.
那條道路通往城市。

road sign 路標

**roar** [ror,rɔr] 動 吼,叫

The lions *roar* when they are angry.
獅子生氣時怒吼。

### roast [rost] 動 烤

Diana is *roasting* a chicken in the fire.
戴安娜正在火邊烤一隻雞。

### rob [rɑb] 動 搶劫，搶奪財物

I was *robbed* last night.
我昨晚被搶劫了。

### robber ['rɑbɚ] 名 盜賊，竊賊

### robbery ['rɑb(ə)rɪ] 名 盜竊，搶劫

There was another *robbery* last night.
昨晚又發生了一起搶劫案。

### robot ['robət,'rɑbət] 名 機器人

The *robot* can talk and walk.
那個機器人會說話，也會走路。

### rock [rɑk] 名 岩石

It's dangerous to climb on the *rocks*.
攀登岩石很危險。

### rocket ['rɑkɪt] 名 火箭

There's nobody in the *rocket*.
那艘火箭裏沒有人。

### roll [rol] 動 滾動，轉動

A big rock is *rolling* down the hill.
一大塊岩石正滾下山來。

### roof [ruf,rʊf] 名 屋頂

The house has a brown *roof*.
那房子的屋頂是棕色的。

### room [rum,rʊm] 名 房間

It's your turn to clean our *room* today.
今天輪到你來打掃房間了。

### root [rut,rʊt] 名 根

Some plants have many *roots*.
有些植物的根鬚很多。

**rope** [rop] 名 繩子
　　Tie the *rope* around the tree.
　　把繩子繫在樹上。

**rose** [roz] 名 玫瑰花
　　They have *roses* in their garden.
　　他們花園裏有玫瑰花。

R

**round** [raʊnd] 形 圓的
　　Is the earth *round*?
　　地球是圓的嗎?

**row** [ro] 名 排,列
　　Dick is in *Row* 4.　迪克在第四排。
　　動 划船
　　They *rowed* boats in the park last Sunday.
　　上星期天他們在公園裏划船。

**rubber** ['rʌbɚ] 名 橡膠,橡皮
　　The car has four *rubber* tires.
　　汽車有四個橡膠輪胎。

**rubbish** ['rʌbɪʃ] 名 垃圾,廢物
　　The workers cleaned the *rubbish* up.
　　工人們清潔了垃圾。

**rude** [r(ɪ)ud] 形 粗魯的,無禮的
　　Don't be *rude* to your mother.
　　不要對你的母親無禮。

**rug** [rʌg] 名 地毯
　　There's a *rug* in front of the door.
　　門前有一塊小地毯。

**rule** [r(ɪ)ul] 名 規則,規定
　　We must obey the school *rules*.
　　我們必須遵守學校規章制度。
　　動 統治
　　The king has *ruled* his country for 20 years.
　　國王已經統治那個國家二十年了。

**ruler** [ˈr(ɪ)ulə] 名 尺

My *ruler* is as long as yours.
我的尺和你的一樣長。

**run** [rʌn] 動 跑，跑步

He warns his grandson not to *run* so fast.
他叮囑他的孫子，不要跑得那麼快。

**rush** [rʌʃ] 動 衝進，衝出

The children *rushed* out of school.
孩子們衝出學校。

**sack** [sæk] 名 袋，包

    Dad bought a *sack* of rice three days ago.

    三天前爸爸買了一袋大米。

**sad** [sæd] 形 悲傷的，沮喪的

    Kate feels very *sad* because her cat died.

    凱特的小貓死了，她非常悲傷。

    反 glad 高興的

**safe** [sef] 形 安全的

    Is it *safe* to go to school alone?

    你獨自一人去上學安全嗎?

    反 dangerous 危險的

**sail** [sel] 動 航行

    The ship will *sail* for
America this afternoon.

    今天下午，這艘船將啟航向美國。

    sailor 船員

**salad** ['sæləd] 名 沙拉

    Put some fruit in the *salad*.

    往沙拉裏放一些水果。

**sale** [sel] 名 出售

    The house is for *sale*.

    那座房子待售。

    salesgirl 女售貨員

**salt** [sɔlt] 名 鹽

**salty** ['sɔltɪ] 形 鹹的

There's little salt in my food. It's not *salty* at all.

我的食物裏幾乎没有鹽，一點也不鹹。

**salute** [sə'l(ɪ)ut] 動 向……敬禮

The pupils are *saluting* the flag.

學生們在向國旗致敬。

**same** [sem] 形 相同的

Sandy and Sue go to the *same* school, but they are in different classes.

桑迪和蘇在同一所學校上學，但不在同一個班。

反 different 不同的

**sand** [sænd] 名 沙子

Let's go and play in the *sand*.

我們到沙灘去玩。

**sandwich** ['sæn(d)wɪtʃ] 名 三明治

Tome likes to eat peanut butter *sandwiches*.

湯姆喜歡吃花生醬三明治。

**Santa Claus** ['sæntə,klɔz,'sæntɪ,klɔz] 名 聖誕老人

*Santa Claus* comes to make all children happy.

聖誕老人的到來使所有的孩子快樂。

**Saturday** ['sætɚdɪ] 名 星期六

*Saturday* is the end of the week.

星期六是周末。

**saucer** ['sɔsɚ] 名 茶碟

Sue put the cup on the *saucer*.

蘇把茶杯放在茶碟上。

**S**

**sausage** ['sɔsɪdʒ,'sɑsɪdʒ] 名 香腸

A *sausage* is made of meat.

香腸是一種肉製品。

**save** [sev] 動 ①救助
②節約

① The little boy was *saved*.

小男孩獲救了。

② *Save* your money.

節約用錢。

**saw** [sɔ] 名 鋸子

The *saw* can cut the wood.

鋸子能夠鋸斷木頭。

**say** [se] 動 說

What did you *say*? 你說了什麼？

説的表示方法

say 說、述說，用言語表達思想； speak 說、講演，講某種語言；

talk 談話、交談; tell 告訴，有傳達講述的意思。

**scarf** [skɑrf] 名 圍巾

Tie the *scarf* around your neck.

戴上你的圍巾。

**school** [skul] 名 學校

He often goes to *school* with a big schoolbag.

他常背著一個大書包去上學。

schoolbag 書包; schoolboy 男學生;

schoolgirl 女學生

**science** ['saɪəns] 名 科學

We learn and use *science*.

我們學科學、用科學。

**scientist** ['saɪəntɪst] 名 科學家

## scissors ['sɪzɚz] 名 剪刀

Here's a new pair of *scissors*.

這是一把新剪刀。

## scold [skold] 動 責備，責罵

The teacher *scolded* Jim for his behavior.

老師責備吉姆的舉止。

## score [skor,skɔr] 名 得分

The *score* is 9 to 5 now. We'll win.

現在比分是 9：5。我們會贏的。

scoreboard 記分牌

## sea [si] 名 海

There are many living things in the *sea*.

海裏有許多生物。

seashore 海岸，海濱

## seaside ['si,saɪd,'si'saɪd] 名 海邊

David wants to buy a house at the *seaside*.

大衛想在海邊買套房。

## season ['sizn̩] 名 季節

The four *seasons* of the year are spring, summer, autumn and winter.

一年中有四個季節：春、夏、秋、冬。

## seat [sit] 名 座位

Don't leave your *seat* during class.

上課時，不要離開座位。

## second ['sɛkənd] 數 第二

The *second* student of the line is Tom.

這排的第二個學生叫湯姆。

名 秒

How many *seconds* are there in an hour?

一小時有多少秒?

**secret** ['sikrɪt] 名 秘密

It's a *secret* between us.
這是我們之間的秘密。

**see** [si] 動 看

What can you *see* in this picture?
在這幅圖裏，你能看見什麼？

**S**

**seed** [sid] 名 種子

This *seed* will grow into a tall plant.
這粒種子將長成一株高大的植物。

**seem** [sim] 動 似乎，好像

It *seems* to be right.
那似乎是正確的。

**sell** [sɛl] 動 賣

The grocer doesn't *sell* vegetables.
那個雜貨商不賣蔬菜。
反 buy 買

**send** [sɛnd] 動 寄，送

Will you *send* me a picture of yourself?
你願意寄一張你的照片給我嗎？

**sense** [sɛns] 名 感官，知覺

I have a good *sense* of hearing.
我的聽覺很敏銳。

**sentence** ['sɛntəns] 名 句子

Our homework is making five *sentences*.
我們的作業是造5個句子。

**September** [sɛp'tɛmbɚ, səp'tɛmbɚ] 名 九月

We go back to school in *September*.
我們九月份返回學校。

tortoise 烏龜

lobster 龍蝦

octopus 章魚

fish
魚

dolphin
海豚

whale 鯨

shark 鯊魚

sea
horse
海馬

sea lion 海獅

conch
海螺

179

## set [sɛt] 動 ①放，置　②落

① He *set* his books on the shelf.
他把書放在架子上。

② The sun is *setting*.
夕陽西下。

反　rise 升起

名 一套

Do you have a *set* of colored pencils?
你有一套彩色筆嗎?

## seven ['sɛvən] 數 七

There are *seven* ducks on the lake.
湖面上有七隻鴨子。

## seventeen [ˌsɛvən'tin, 'sɛvən'tin] 數 十七

Can you count to *seventeen* in English?
你能用英語數到17嗎?

## seventy ['sɛvəntɪ] 數 七十

Is your grandfather *seventy* years old?
你爺爺70歲了嗎?

## several ['sɛv(ə)rəl] 形 幾個

There are *several* butterflies in the garden.
花園裏有幾隻蝴蝶。

## sew [so] 動 縫補

I'm learning to *sew* a dress.
我正在學縫衣服。

## shade [ʃed] 名 樹蔭，蔭影

We took a rest in the *shade* of the tree.
我們在樹蔭下休息了一會。

## shadow ['ʃædo, 'ʃædə] 名 影子

I can see my *shadow*.
我能看見我的影子。

**shake** [ʃek] 動 搖動、抖動

Do you *shake* hands with your teacher?

你和你的老師握手嗎?

**shall** [ʃæl,弱 ʃəl] 助動 ①將要 ②……好嗎

① I *shall* come back in July.

我將在七月份回來。

② *Shall* we go to the Water Park?

我們去水上公園好嗎?

**shallow** [ˈʃælo,ˈʃælə] 形 淺的

Mike is walking into the *shallow* water.

邁克在淺水中行走。

反 deep 深的

**shape** [ʃep] 名 形狀

Different things have different *shapes*.

不同的物體有不同的形狀。

**share** [ʃɛr,ʃær] 動 分享

I *shared* my cookies with my classmates.

我把餅乾分給同學一起吃。

**sharp** [ʃɑrp] 形 鋒利的,尖銳的

The knife is very *sharp*.

這把刀非常鋒利。

反 dull 鈍的

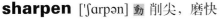

**sharpen** [ˈʃɑrpən] 動 削尖,磨快

*Sharpen* this pencil, please.

請削尖這枝鉛筆。

**shave** [ʃev] 動 刮,剃

Father *shaves* his face every morning.

爸爸每天早上刮臉。

## she [ʃi,弱ʃɪ] 代 她

*She* is a nice girl.
她是一個好女孩。
*She* repaired it herself.
她自己修好了。

## sheep [ʃip] 名 羊

The *sheep* is eating grass.
那隻羊在吃草。

## sheet [ʃit] 名 ①一張，一塊　②被單，褥單

① Write your homework on a *sheet* of paper.
把作業寫在一張紙上。

② Don't make the *sheet* dirty.
別把床單弄髒了。

## shelf [ʃɛlf] 名 架子

There are two newspapers on the *shelf*.
架子上有兩張報紙。

## shell [ʃɛl] 名 殼，甲殼，外殼

I found this *shell* at the beach.
我在沙灘上找到這枚貝殼。

## shine [ʃaɪn] 動 照耀，閃耀

The lights *shine* brightly.
電燈照得很亮。

## ship [ʃɪp] 名 船

Have you traveled by *ship*?
你坐船旅行過嗎?

## shirt [ʃɝt] 名 襯衫

Tom wears his father's *shirt* and shoes.
湯姆穿著爸爸的襯衫和鞋。
T-shirt　T恤衫

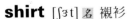

**shoe** [ʃu,ʃıu] 名 鞋

The *shoes* are too big for him.
這雙鞋對他來說太大了。

**shoot** [ʃut] 動 射擊

Jim wants to *shoot* with his gun.
吉姆想用槍射擊。

**shop** [ʃɑp] 名 商店

Jack went into the flower *shop*.
傑克走進了那家花店。

**shopping** ['ʃɑpıŋ] 動 購物

Can I go *shopping* with you, Mom?
我和你一起去購物好嗎，媽媽？

shopping-list 購物單

**short** [ʃɔrt] 形 ①短的　②矮的

① This pen is long and that one is *short*.
這枝筆長，那枝筆短。

反　long 長的

② Who is the *shortest* in your class?
在你們班裏，誰個子最矮？

反　tall 高的

**shorts** [ʃɔrts] 名 短褲

He wears blue *shorts*.
他穿著藍短褲。

**should** [ʃʊd,弱 ʃəd] 助動 應該

You *should* say "sorry" to her.
你應該對她說聲對不起。

**shoulder** ['ʃoldɚ] 名 肩膀

His shoulder is very broad.
他的肩膀很寬。

### shout [ʃaʊt] 動 呼喊，喊叫

Don't *shout* at her.
不要對著她大聲喊叫。

### shovel [ˈʃʌvl̩] 名 鏟，鐵鍬

Dick wants to dig a hole with the *shovel*.
迪克想用鐵鍬挖一個坑。

### show [ʃo] 動 出示，展示

The pictures *show* real life back then.
這些照片顯示了當時的真實生活。

### shower [ˈʃaʊɚˌˈʃaʊr] 名 ①淋浴　②陣雨

① Tom is taking a *shower*.
　湯姆在洗淋浴。
② The *shower* is coming.
　要下陣雨了。

### shut [ʃʌt] 動 關，閉

Please *shut* the door.
請關門。
同　close 關
反　open 開

### shy [ʃaɪ] 形 害羞的

He's too *shy* to talk with us.
他太害羞了，不敢和我們講話。

### sick [sɪk] 形 生病的

Mother made a lot of good food for me when I was *sick*.
我生病的時候，媽媽爲我做了許多好吃的。
反　healthy 健康的

### side [saɪd] 名 邊，側面

There are trees on both *sides* of the road.
道路兩邊都是樹。

**sight** [saɪt] 名 視力

A man must have good *sight* to drive.

開車的人必須要有好視力。

**sign** [saɪn] 名 標誌，符號

Obey the road *signs*.

遵守交通標誌。

動 簽名

*Sign* your name in this book, please.

請在這本書上簽上你的名字。

**silence** ['saɪləns] 名 沉默

We should listen to the teacher in *silence*.

我們應該靜靜地聽老師講課。

**silent** ['saɪlənt] 形 沉默的

Don't be *silent*. Teli me your ideas.

不要沉默，告訴我我的想法。

反 noisy 吵鬧的

**silk** [sɪlk] 名 絲綢

The blouse is made of *silk*.

那件罩衫是用絲綢做的。

**silly** ['sɪlɪ] 形 愚蠢的

I am so *silly*! I put it in my pocket.

我多傻啊！我把它放在口袋裏了。

同 foolish 愚蠢的

反 wise 聰明的

**silver** ['sɪlvɚ] 名 銀

I have a *silver* ring.

我有一枚銀戒指。

**simple** ['sɪmpḷ] 形 簡單的，簡易的

These questions are all *simple*.

這些問題都很簡單。

## since [sɪns] 介 連 自從

It's two years *since* I left my hometown.
我離開家鄉已經兩年了。

副 從那以後，後來

I haven't seen her *since* last Thursday.
自上星期四以來，我一直沒有見過他。

## sing [sɪŋ] 動 唱歌

They are *singing*.
他們在唱歌。

## singer ['sɪŋɚ] 名 歌手，歌唱家

## sink [sɪŋk] 動 下沉

The ship *sank* in the sea.
那艘輪船沉入大海。

## sir [sɝ, 弱 sɚ] 名 先生

I'm sorry, *sir*.
對不起，先生。

## sister ['sɪstɚ] 名 姐妹

Lucy is Peter's *sister*.
露茜是彼得的妹妹。

sister-in-law 嫂子；elder sister 姐姐；younger sister 妹妹

## sit [sɪt] 坐 動

*Sit* up, children.
坐正，孩子們。
*Sit* down, please.
請坐。

sitting-room 起居室
反 stand 站

## six [sɪks] 數 六

— What's five plus one?
5 加 1 等於幾？

— *Six*.
等於 6。

**sixteen** [sɪks'tin,'sɪks'tin] 數 十六

Tom's schoolbag costs *sixteen* dollars.

湯姆的書包值16美元。

**sixty** ['sɪkstɪ] 數 六十

My grandmother is over *sixty*.

我奶奶60多歲了。

**size** [saɪz] 名 尺寸，尺碼

—What *size* are your shoes?

你的鞋是多大尺寸？

—*Size* 36.

三十六碼。

**skate** [sket] 動 滑冰

Dick is *skating* on the lake.

迪克在湖面上滑冰。

**ski** [ski] 動 滑雪

Jim learned to *ski* during his vacation.

吉姆在假期學會了滑雪。

**skin** [skɪn] 名 皮膚

We have yellow *skin*.

我們是黃皮膚。

**skirt** [skɜt] 名 裙子

These girls all wear *skirts*.

這些女孩都穿著裙子。

**sky** [skaɪ] 名 天空

How many birds are there in the *sky*?

天空中有多少隻鳥？

**sleep** [slip] 動 睡覺

Kate is *sleeping*.

凱特正在睡覺。

**sleepy**

## sleepy ['slipɪ] 形 瞌睡的、想睡的

Nobody looks *sleepy* although it's eleven thirty.
儘管已經十一點半了，但是沒有人看起來想睡覺。

### sleeve [sliv] 名 袖子

She likes to wear short *sleeve* coat.
她喜歡穿短袖上衣。

### slice [slaɪs] 名 片，塊

Take several *slices* of bread to Sandy.
給桑迪拿幾片麵包。

## slide [slaɪd] 名 滑梯

The children are playing on the *slide*.
孩子們在溜滑梯。

### slip [slɪp] 動 滑倒

Jim *slipped* on the ice.
吉姆在冰上滑倒了。

### slipper ['slɪpə] 名 拖鞋

We wear *slippers* at home.
我們在家穿拖鞋。

## slippery ['slɪp(ə)rɪ] 形 光滑的，滑溜的

Ice made the path *slippery*.
冰使得小路變滑。

### slot [slɑt] 名 小孔，小槽

You can put money through the *slot*.
你可以通過小槽把錢放進去。

## slow [slo] 形 慢的

The clock is two minutes *slow*.
那隻錶慢兩分鐘。

## slowly ['slolɪ] 副 慢地

The teacher asked us to sit down *slowly*.
老師要我們慢慢地坐下。

**small** [smɔl] 形 小的

The chair and desk are too *small*.

那桌椅太小了。

反 big 大的

**smart** [smɑrt] 形 聰明的，精明的

She's a *smart* girl.

她是個聰明的女孩。

**smell** [smɛl] 動 聞

The flower *smells* good.

這枝花聞起來很香。

名 氣味

Do you like the *smell* of onions?

你喜歡洋蔥的氣味嗎?

**smile** [smaɪl] 動 微笑

The girl *smiled* at me.

那個女孩對著我微笑。

名 微笑

There's always a *smile* on Miss Wu's face.

吳老師的臉上總掛著微笑。

**smoke** [smok] 動 抽煙

Mr. White doesn't *smoke*.

懷特先生不抽煙。

No *smoking*.

禁止抽煙。

名 煙

A lot of *smoke* is coming out of the chimney.

從煙囪中冒出一縷濃煙。

**smooth** [smuð] 形 ①光滑的　②平整的

① The cloth feels *smooth*.

這布料摸起來光滑。

② Go along the *smooth* road.

沿著平坦的道路前行。

## snail [snel] 名 蝸牛

A *snail* carries a shell on its back.
蝸牛背上背著一個殼。

## snake [snek] 名 蛇

Some people eat *snakes*.
有些人吃蛇。

### sneaker ['s] 名 運動鞋

This pair of *sneakers* is too small for me.
這雙運動鞋對我來說太小了。

### snow [sno] 名 雪

We had a heavy *snow* yesterday.
昨天下了一場大雪。

動 下雪
It's still *snowing*.
雪還在下。

snowball 雪球; snowman 雪人

## so [so] 副 這麼，如此

Don't be *so* naughty, Mike.
邁克，別這麼淘氣。

語法
用在 believe, hope, say, tell ,do 等之後，避免重覆。
"Is he coming?" "I hope *so*."
"他會來嗎？" "我希望會來。"

連 因此，所以
It was hot *so* I turned on the fan.
天氣太熱，所以我打開了電扇。

### soap [sop] 名 香皂，肥皂

Wash your hands with *soap*.
用肥皂洗洗你的手。

### sock [sak] 名 短襪

Take off your dirty *socks and wash them*.
脫掉你的髒襪子，去洗一洗。

# sofa ['sofə] 名 沙發

Sit on the *sofa* and have a rest, please.
請坐在沙發上歇一會。

## soft [sɔft] 形 ①軟的
②温柔的

① The rabbit is *soft* to touch.
小兔子摸起來是柔軟的。

反 hard 硬的

② Betty speaks in a *soft* voice.
貝蒂説話聲音很柔。

# soldier ['soldʒɚ] 名 士兵，軍人

*Soldiers* must obey their officers.
軍人必須服從上級的命令。

## some [sʌm,弱 səm] 形名 一些

There are *some* apples in the bowl.
碗裏有一些蘋果。

Would you like *some* orange juice?
你想要些橙汁嗎?

# somebody ['sʌmbɑdɪ,'sʌm,bʌdɪ] 代 某人，有人

*Somebody* is standing beside that box.
有人站在那個盒子旁邊。

someone = somebody

# something ['sʌmθɪŋ, 'sʌmpθɪŋ] 名 某事，某物

I have *something* to tell you.
我有些事要告訴你。

I'd like *something* to drink.
我想要些喝的東西。

# sometimes ['sʌm,taɪmz,səm'taɪmz] 副 有時候

*Sometimes* I'm careless, too.
有時，我也很粗心。

**son** [sʌn] 名 兒子

He carries his *son* on his shoulders.
他把兒子扛在肩上。

**song** [sɔŋ] 名 歌

My teacher can sing Japanese *songs*.
我的老師會唱日語歌。

**soon** [sun,sʊn] 副 不久，馬上

It will be a new year *soon*.
新的一年馬上就要到了。

**sorry** ['sɑrɪ,'sɔrɪ] 形 ①抱歉的　②難過的

① "I'm *sorry*, Miss Williams."
"That's all right."
"對不起，威廉姆斯小姐。"
"沒關係。"

② I'm *sorry* to hear the bad news.
聽到這個壞消息,我很難過。

反　glad 高興的

**sound** [saʊnd] 名 聲音

We hear *sounds* with our ears.
我們用耳朵聽聲音。

**soup** [sup] 名 湯

I had tomato *soup* for lunch.
我午餐喝的是蕃茄湯。

**sour** ['saʊr] 形 酸的

The lemon is very *sour*.
這個檸檬很酸。

反　sweet　甜的

### south [sauθ] 名 南方

On a map, *south* is at the bottom.
在地圖上，南方在下端。

形 南方的
A warm *south* wind is blowing.
一陣溫暖的南風吹來。

副 向南方，在南方
The dog runs *south*.
那狗向南跑走了。

## space [spes] 名 太空

Man has explored *space* for years.
人類探索太空已有多年了。

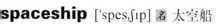

## spaceship ['spes,ʃɪp] 名 太空船

## speak [spik] 動 講話，説話

Do you *speak* English?
你會講英語嗎？

## special ['spɛʃəl] 形 特別的，特殊的

Your birthday is a *special* day for you.
你的生日對你來説是一個特別的日子。

## speed [spid] 名 速度

The *speed* of the bus is 40 kilometers an hour.
這輛公共汽車的時速是40公里。

## spell [spɛl] 動 拼寫

Can you *spell* your English name?
你會拼寫你的英文名字嗎？

## spend [spɛnd] 動 ①花費 ②度過

① Jim has *spent* all his money.
　　吉姆花完了所有的錢。

反　earn 賺錢

② He *spent* a whole day in the market.
　　他在市場上度過一整天。

**spider** ['spaɪdɚ] 名 蜘蛛

Are you afraid of *spiders*?
你害怕蜘蛛嗎?

**spit** [spɪt] 動 吐痰
No spitting!
不准隨地吐痰!

**spoil** [spɔɪl] 動 溺愛,寵壞
Billy's parents *spoil* him.
比利的父母寵壞了他。

**spoon** [spun,spʊn] 名 湯匙
Jane is eating soup with a *spoon*.
珍正在用湯匙喝湯。

**sport** [sport,spɔrt] 名 運動
We play a lot of *sports*.
我們做各種運動。

**spring** [sprɪŋ] 名 春天
In the *spring*, plants start to grow.
植物在春天開始生長。

**square** [skwɛr] 名 正方形
A *square* has four equal sides.
正方形有四條相等的邊。

**squirrel** ['skwɝəl] 名 松鼠
A *squirrel* loves to eat nuts.
松鼠喜歡吃堅果。

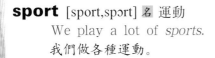

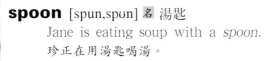

**stadium** ['stedɪəm] 名 運動場,體育場
They are watching the match in the *stadium*.
他們在體育場內觀看比賽。

**stair** [stɛr,stær] 名 階梯，樓梯

Don't play on the *stairs*, boys!

孩子們，別在樓梯上玩耍！

**stamp** [stæmp] 名 郵票

Don't forget to put a *stamp* on the envelope.

別忘了在信封上貼上郵票。

**stand** [stænd] 動 站

Tom *stood* in front of the door for a long time.

湯姆在門前站了好久了。

**star** [stɑr] 名 星

The sky is full of *stars* tonight.

今夜星光滿天。

**start** [stɑrt] 動 ①出發 ②開始

① Let's *start* at three o'clock.

我們三點鐘出發吧。

② The football match will *start* at seven o'clock tonight.

足球比賽將在今晚 7 點鐘開始。

反 end 結束

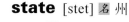

**state** [stet] 名 州

How many *states* are there in America?

美國有多少個州？

**station** ['steʃən] 名 車站

Sandy and Sue will meet at the *station* tomorrow.

桑迪和蘇明天將在車站會面。

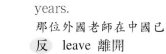

**stay** [ste] 動 停留，逗留

The foreign teacher has *stayed* in China for two years.

那位外國老師在中國已經待了兩年。

反 leave 離開

### steak [stek] 名 牛排

Peter ate *steak* at his aunt's this morning.

彼得今天早上在姨媽家吃牛排。

### steal [stil] 動 偷

Someone has *stolen* Jane's pen.

有人偷走了珍的鋼筆。

## steam [stim] 名 蒸汽，汽

When water gets to 100°C, it boils and becomes *steam*.

水溫達到100攝氏度時，水會沸騰而變成水蒸氣。

## steel [stil] 名 鋼

All these things are made of *steel*.

這些東西都是鋼製的。

## step [stɛp] 名 ①步，腳步 ②臺階

① Take a *step* forward.

向前走一步。

② Mind the *steps*!

當心臺階！

### stick [stɪk] 名 棍，棒

The dog has a *stick* in its mouth.

那隻狗嘴裡叼著一根木棒。

### still [stɪl] 副 仍然，還

Mother is *still* making a shopping list.

媽媽還在寫購物單。

## sting [stɪŋ] 動 叮，刺，螫

I got *stung* by a bee yesterday.

昨天蜜蜂螫了我一下。

## stir [stɝ] 動 攪拌

Kate is *stirring* the soup slowly.

凱特在慢慢地攪湯。

### **stocking** ['stɑkɪŋ] 名 長筒襪

Alice wears a pair of *stocking*s.

艾麗斯穿著一雙長筒襪。

### **stomach** ['stʌmək] 名 胃

The food we eat goes into our *stomach*.

我們吃的食物進入我們的胃部。

## **stomachache** ['stʌmək,ek] 名 胃疼,肚子痛

Tom has got a *stomachache*.

湯姆肚子痛。

## **stone** [ston] 名 石頭

Some *stone*s are big, some are small.

有些石頭大，有些石頭小。

### **stool** [stul] 名 凳子

Sit on the *stool*, please.

請坐在那個凳子上。

### **stop** [stɑp] 動 停止

*Stop* talking, children.

孩子們，停止說話。

*Stop* to talk, children.

孩子們，停下來說話。

反 begin 開始

## **store** [stor,stɔr] 名 商場，商店

There's a furniture *store* near the park.

公園附近有一個家具商場。

同 shop 商店

## **storeroom** ['stor,rʊm,'stɔr,rʊm,'stɔr,rum] 名 貯藏室

## **storm** [stɔrm] 名 暴風雨

The sky becomes dark and the wind blows hard when a *storm* is coming.

暴風雨來臨時，天空變暗，風力加強。

**story** ['storɪ,'stɔrɪ] 名 故事

Mr. Wang tells his son a *story* every evening.
王先生每天晚上為兒子講一個故事。

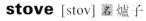

**stove** [stov] 名 爐子

I can't move the *stove* in the kitchen.
我移不動廚房的爐子。

**straight** [stret] 形 直的

Draw a *straight* line from A to B.
從 A 到 B 之間畫一條直線。
反 bent 彎曲

**strange** [strendʒ] 形 ①奇怪的　②陌生的

① It's *strange!* It's empty!
　　　這怎麼空了！
② A *strange* man is coming over to me.
　　一個陌生人向我走來。

**straw** [strɔ] 名①吸管　②稻草

① You can drink through the *straw*.
　　你可以用吸管喝。
② Put the *straw* in the barn.
　　把稻草堆到牲口棚裏。

**strawberry** ['strɔ,bɛrɪ,'strɔ,bərɪ] 名 草莓

**street** [strit] 名 街道

What's the name of the *street*?
這條街的名字是什麼？

**strict** [strɪkt] 形 嚴厲的

Mr. Yang is very *strict* with us.
楊老師對我們要求非常嚴格。

**string** [strɪŋ] 名 細繩，線

John tied up the parcel with *string*.
約翰用細繩把包裹捆好。

**stripe** [straɪp] 名 條紋

Jack wears a tie with black and red *stripes*.
傑克戴著一條紅黑條紋相間的領帶。

**strong** [strɔŋ] 形 強壯的

A *strong* man can lift the big stone.
一個強壯的人能將這塊大石頭舉起來。

反 weak 軟弱的

**student** ['stjudṇt,'st(ɪ)udṇt] 名 學生

Mike's cousin is a middle school *student*.
邁克的堂兄是個中學生。

**study** ['stʌdɪ] 動 學習

Everyone *studies* harder before the examination.
每個人在考試前都更加努力地學習。

比較

study 含有研究的性質，強調深入的、較高深的學習。learn 學、
學會，側重初級階段或帶有模仿性的學習。

**stupid** ['stjupɪd,'st(ɪ)upɪd] 形 愚蠢的，笨的

What a *stupid* thing you did!
你做了一件多麼愚蠢的事啊！

反 bright 聰明的

**subject** ['sʌbdʒɪkt] 名 學科，科目

What *subject* do you like best?
你最喜歡什麼科目？

**subway** ['sʌb,we] 名 (美) 地鐵

Should we go by *subway*?
我們乘地鐵去好嗎?

同 underground （英）地鐵

**succeed** [sək'sid] 動 成功

I believe that you will *succeed*.
我相信你會成功的。

反 fail 失敗

**success** [sək'sɛs] 名 成功

Success comes from hard work.

成功來自於努力地工作。

反 failure 失敗

**such** [sʌtʃ,弱 sətʃ] 代 ①如此，這樣

②這樣的人(物)，這樣的事

① Such was the fact.

事實就是如此。

② I have never seen such a big pig.

我從沒見過這麼大的豬。

**suddenly** ['sʌdn̩lɪ] 副 突然地

Suddenly I heard the fierce barks.

突然間，我聽到幾聲狂吠聲。

**sugar** ['ʃʊgɚ] 名 糖

Sandy put some sugar in his milk.

桑迪在他的牛奶裏放了一些糖。

**suit** [sut,sjut,sɪut] 動 適合

The sunglasses don't suit you very well.

這太陽鏡不太適合你。

名 套裝，套裙

Wear a suit to the interview.

會面時穿上西裝。

**sum** [sʌm] 名 和，總數

The sum of eight and nine is seventeen.

8和9的和是17。

**summer** ['sʌmɚ] 名 夏天

We can eat many fresh vegetables and fruit in summer.

夏天,我們可以吃到許多新鮮的蔬菜瓜果。

## sun [sʌn] 名 太陽

Don't read in the *sun*.

不要在陽光下看書。

*sunflower* 向日葵; sunset 日落; sunlight 太陽光

# Sunday ['sʌndɪ] 名 星期日

Many people do not go to work on *Sunday*.

許多人星期天不上班。

星期的表達

Sunday 星期日; Monday 星期一; Tuesday 星期二;

Wednesday 星期三; Thursday 星期四; Friday 星期五;

Saturday 星期六; weekday 平日（星期一到星期五）;

weekend 周末（星期六和星期日）

### sunny ['sʌnɪ] 形 陽光明媚的

Great! It's *sunny* today.

太棒了，今天是晴天。

### supermarket ['supɚ,mɑrkɪt] 名 超級市場

We can buy all kinds of things in the *supermarket*.

我們能在超級市場裏買到各種各樣的東西。

## supper ['sʌpɚ] 名 晚餐

Diana is making *supper*.

戴安娜正在做晚餐。

## suppose [sə'poz] 動 假設，猜想

*Suppose* it rained, would we still go?

假使下雨的話，我們還去嗎？

## sure [ʃʊr] 形 確信的，確定的

Are you *sure* that's Jim?

你確信他是吉姆嗎？

## surprise [sə'praɪz,sə'praɪz] 動 驚奇

The news *surprised* me. (I'm *surprised* at the news.)
那消息令我感到驚奇。

## sweater ['swɛtɚ] 名 毛衣

My aunt bought a new *sweater* for me.
我的姑姑爲我買了件新毛衣。

## sweep [swip] 動 掃除

We *sweep* our classroom every day.
我們每天都打掃教室。

## sweet [swit] 名 糖果

Billy has ten *sweets*, Sandy has only two.
比利有十塊糖，桑迪只有兩塊。

形 甜的

Sugar and honey are both *sweet*.
糖和蜂蜜都是甜的。

味覺表達詞

sour 酸的; sweet 甜的; bitter 苦的; hot 辣的; salty 鹹的

## swim [swɪm] 動 游泳

Jim *swims* like a fish.
吉姆游得像魚一樣靈活。
swim suit 女泳裝

## swing [swɪŋ] 名 鞦韆

Lucy is sitting on the *swing*.
露西正坐在鞦韆上。

## switch [swɪtʃ] 名 開關

The light *switch* is near the door. Press it, please.
燈的開關在門旁邊。請按一下。

## sword [sord,sɔrd] 名 劍

The man drew his *sword*.
那個男人拔出了劍。

**table** ['tebl] 名 桌子
Put the food on the *table*.
把食物放在桌子上。
tablecloth 桌布，臺布

**tablet** ['tæblɪt] 名 藥片，藥丸
Take two of the *tablets* before meals.
每頓飯前服兩粒藥片。

**tail** [tel] 名 尾巴
A rabbit has a short *tail*.
兔子的尾巴短。
heads or tails 正面還是反面(擲錢幣)

**tailor** ['telɚ] 名 裁縫
She is a good *tailor*.
她是一個好裁縫。

**take** [tek] 動 ①拿，取 ②乘

① *Take* this coat to your aunt, Rose.
羅斯，把這件衣服帶給你姨媽。
② She *took* a bus to her aunt's.
她乘公共汽車去姑姑家。

比較

take, bring, fetch: take 強調 "帶走，拿走"; bring 強調 "帶來，拿來";
fetch 強調 "去取來，走拿來"，表示到別處取了後再返回來。

**talk** [tɔk] 動 談話，説話

Mary is *talking* with her friend.
瑪麗正在和她的朋友説話。

**tall** [tɔl] 形 高的，一定高度的

The child is *tall*.
那個孩子很高。

He's one and a half meters *tall*.
他身高 1.5 米。

**tame** [tem] 形 馴服的，温順的

The cat and the dog are both *tame*.
那隻貓和那條狗都被馴服了。

反　wild 野的，野蠻的

**tap** [tæp] 名 水龍頭

Turn off the *tap*, Sandy.
桑迪，關掉水龍頭。

動 輕擊，輕敲

Don't *tap* on the glass.
不要在玻璃杯上敲。

**tape** [tep] 名 磁帶，錄音帶

Let's listen to the *tape* of the text.
讓我們來聽一下課文錄音。

**taste** [test] 動 品嘗

*Taste* it, please.
請嘗一嘗。

名 味道

Do you like the *taste* of this cake?
你喜歡這種蛋糕的味道嗎?

**taxi** ['tæksɪ] 名 計程車

We'll take a *taxi* to the station.
我們將搭計程車去車站。

**T**

陸上交通工具

bicycle 自行車；　motorcycle 摩托車；　car 小汽車；　bus 公共汽車；
truck 卡車；　tractor 拖拉機；　jeep 吉普車；　taxi 計程車；　train 火車

## tea [ti] 名 茶

The Chinese like to drink *tea*.
中國人喜歡喝茶。
teacup 茶杯；　teapot 茶壺

## teach [titʃ] 動 教

Miss Williams *teaches* them math.
威廉斯小姐教他們數學。
反　learn 學習

## teacher [titʃɚ] 名 老師

My mother is my first *teacher*.
媽媽是我的第一任老師。

## team [tim] 名 隊，組

Our *team* won the game.
我們隊贏了比賽。

## tear [tɛr,tær] 動 撕，扯

Mary *tore* the letter into pieces.
瑪麗把信撕成了碎片。

### tear [tɪr] 名 眼淚

Her eyes are full of *tears*.
她的眼裏盈滿了淚水。

### telephone ['tɛlə,fon] 名 電話

I spoke to him on the *telephone* today.
今天我和他通了電話。

## telescope ['tɛlə,skop] 名 望遠鏡

Sandy is looking through the *telescope*.
桑迪正在用望遠鏡觀看。

**television** ['tɛləˌvɪʒən] 名 電視

There's something wrong with the *television*.
電視機出了毛病。

縮 TV

**tell** [tɛl] 動 告訴，講述

*Tell* me about your family.
跟我談談你的家庭。

**temperature** ['tɛmp(ə)rətʃɚ] 名 溫度

What's the *temperature* today?
今天的氣溫是多少?

**temple** ['tɛmpl̩] 名 廟宇

Many people pray in the *temple*.
許多人在廟裏禱告。

**ten** [tɛn] 數 十

There are *ten* classrooms on this floor.
這層樓上有十間教室。

**tennis** ['tɛnɪs] 名 網球

Peter and Jim are playing *tennis*.
彼得和吉姆在打網球。

**tent** [tɛnt] 名 帳篷

The boys put up the *tent* quickly.
男孩子們很快搭起了帳篷。

**term** [tɝm] 名 學期

A school year is divided into two *terms*.
一學年被分成兩個學期。

**terrible** ['tɛrəbl̩] 形 ①可怕的 ②極壞的，很糟的

① It was a *terrible* accident.
那是一次極可怕的事故。

② I'm *terrible* at ping-pong.
我乒乓球打得很糟。

**test** [tɛst] 名 考試，測驗
They are taking a *test*.
他們正在進行一次考試。

**text** [tɛkst] 名 課文
Read the *text*, please.
請讀一下課文。

**T**

**than** [ðæn, 弱 ðən] 副 連 比，比較
Sue plays better *than* Sandy does.
蘇彈奏得比桑迪好。
Sue is older *than* Sandy.
蘇比桑迪年齡大。

**thank** [θæŋk] 動 感謝
"*Thank* you very much."
"太謝謝你了。"
"You're welcome."
"別客氣。"
Thanks.= Thank you.

**that** [ðæt, ðət] 形 代 那，那個
*That*'s Jim.
那是吉姆。
*That* engineer is my uncle.
那名工程師是我的叔叔。

**the** [ði, 弱 ðə] 冠 這，那
David has a car. *The* car is black.
大衛有一輛汽車。那車是黑色的。

**theater** ['θiətɚ, 'θɪətɚ] 名 劇院
The village has an open-air *theater*.
那個村子裏有一個露天劇場。

**then** [ðεn] 副 ①當時　②然後

①　Where were they *then*?

當時他們在哪兒?

反　now 現在

②　First we had dinner, *then* we watched TV.

我們先吃晚飯、然後看電視。

**there** [ðεr,ðær] 副 ①在那裏，往那裏　②‧(與動詞 be 連用)

①　My bicycle is over *there*.

我的腳踏車在那兒。

反　here 這裏

②　*There are* some geese in the river.

河裏有幾隻鵝。

*There is* some soup in the bowl.

碗裏有一些湯。

**these** [ðiz] 代形 這些

*These* are my books.

這些是我的書。

*These* books are mine.

這些書是我的。

反　those 那些

**they** [ðe,弱 ðε,ðɪ] 代 他們

*They* are my friends.

他們是我的朋友。

I often play with *them*.

我經常與他們一起玩耍。

*Their* books are on the ground.

他們的書在地上。

The clothes are also *theirs*.

那衣服也是他們的。

*They* cook by *themselves*.

他們自己做飯。

### thick [θɪk] 形 厚的

These dictionaries are very *thick*.

這些辭典非常厚。

反 thin 薄的

### thief [θif] 名 賊，小偷

Two *thieves* broke into our neighbour's house last night.

昨晚，有兩個小偷偷了我們鄰居家。

### thin [θɪn] 形 ①瘦的 ②薄的 ③細的

① The boy is tall and rather *thin*.

這個男孩又高又瘦。

② This book is very *thin*.

這本書很薄。

③ This is a *thin* rope.

這是一條細繩子。

### thing [θɪŋ] 名 東西，物品

Some girls are afraid of eating sweet *thing*s.

有些女孩害怕吃甜東西。

### think [θɪŋk] 動 想，考慮

What's Lucy *thinking* about?

露茜在想什麼呢？

### third [θɜd] 數 第三

The *third* balloon is Helen's.

第三個氣球是海倫的。

### thirsty ['θɜstɪ] 形 渴的

The dog is *thirsty*.

狗渴了。

### thirteen [θɜ'tin] 數 十三

*Thirteen* is an unlucky number in some western countries.

在一些西方國家裏，13被當作一個不吉利的數字。

**thirty** ['θɜtɪ] 數 三十
There are *thirty* days in this month.
這個月有三十天。

**this** [ðɪs] 形 代 這，這個
*This* is an English book.
這是一本英語書。
*This* car is Mr. White's.
這輛車是懷特先生的。
反 that 那個

**thorn** [θɔrn] 名 刺
Don't touch the *thorns* on the rose.
不要去碰玫瑰花上的刺。

**those** [ðoz] 代形 那些
*Those* are your books.
那些是你的書。
*Those* books are yours.
那些書是你的。

**though** [ðo] 連 雖然，儘管
*Though* I studied hard, I failed the test.
儘管我努力學習，但是我仍然沒有及格。

**thousand** ['θaʊzn̩(d)] 數 千
One *thousand* five hundred people live in the village.
那個村裏住了一千五百人。

**thread** [θrɛd] 名 線
Kate used blue *thread*.
凱特用的是藍線。

**three** [θri] 數 三
*Three* students are studying.
三個學生在學習。

**throat** [θrot] 名 喉嚨

Kate had a cold and a sore *throat*.
凱特感冒了，喉嚨也痛。

**through** [θr(ı)u] 介 通過

The puppy goes *through* the big steel pipe.
小狗從大鋼管裏穿過。

**throw** [θro] 動 扔

Jack is ready to *throw* the rope.
傑克準備扔繩子。

**thumb** [θʌm] 名 拇指

Pick up the matches with your *thumb* and finger.
用拇指和食指把火柴撿起來。

**thunder** ['θʌndɚ] 名 雷，雷聲

Did you hear the *thunder* last night?
昨晚你聽到雷聲了嗎?

**Thursday** ['θɝzdı] 名 星期四

The basketball game is on *Thursday*.
籃球賽將在星期四舉行。

**ticket** ['tıkıt] 名 票，入場券

Sue bought a *ticket* before she got on the train.
蘇上火車前買了一張票。
raffle ticket 彩票

**tickle** ['tıkl] 動 使發癢

Mike *tickled* Billy's nose with hair.
邁克用頭髮把比利的鼻子弄得癢癢的。

**tidy** ['taıdı] 形 整齊的，整潔的

Teachers like *tidy* work.
老師喜歡整齊的作業。

tie

**tie** [taɪ] 名 領帶

Whose *tie* is this?

這是誰的領帶?

**tiger** ['taɪgɚ] 名 老虎

We can see *tigers* in the zoo.

我們在那個動物園裏能看到老虎。

**tight** [taɪt] 形 緊的，牢固的

The knot is too *tight*, I can't undo it.

這個結太緊了，我解不開它。

反　loose　鬆的

**till** [tɪl] 介連 直到

They play outdoors *till* it's dark.

他們在戶外一直玩到天黑。

He didn't see her *till* the next day.

他直到第二天才見到她。

**time** [taɪm] 名 時間

What *time* is it? = What's the *time*?

幾點了?

**tin** [tɪn] 名 ①錫　②罐頭盒

① This can is made of *tin*.

這個罐子是由錫製成的。

② It's a *tin* of cookies.

那是一罐餅乾。

**tip** [tɪp] 名 尖端

The *tip* of the pencil is sharp.

這枝鉛筆頭很尖。

**tire** ['taɪr] 名 輪胎　(=tyre)

David bought two *tires* for his car.

大衛為他的汽車買了兩個新輪胎。

**tired** ['taɪrd] 形 疲勞的，累的

Diana feels *tired* after working all day.

戴安娜工作了一整天感到很累。

**to** [tu,弱 tʊ,tə] 介 到，往，向

Dad, will you take me *to* the park on Sunday?

爸爸，你星期天能帶我去公園嗎？

Sue walked *to* the door slowly.

蘇慢慢地向門走去。

用法

to+ 動詞原形，構成不定式

They went *to* get their bags.

他們去拿書包。

**today** [tə'de] 名副 今天

What day is it *today*?

今天是星期幾？

*Today* is Sunday.

今天是星期天。

No one will come *today*.

今天沒有人會來。

**toe** [to] 名 腳趾

What's wrong with your big *toe*?

你的大腳趾怎麼啦？

**together** [tə'gɛðɚ] 副 一起

Our class went to see the exhibition *together*.

我們全班同學一起去看展覽。

**tomato** [tə'meto,tə'metə] 名 西紅柿，蕃茄

There is only one *tomato* left.

只剩下一個蕃茄了。

**tomorrow** [tə'mɔro,tə'maro] 名副 明天

*Tomorrow* is Children's Day.

明天是兒童節。

## tongue [tʌŋ] 名 舌頭

He's tasting the ice cream with his *tongue*.
他正在用舌頭嘗冰淇淋。

## tonight [tə'naɪt] 名副 今晚

It's going to rain *tonight*.
今晚要下雨。
You'd better go to bed early *tonight*.
你今晚最好早點睡覺。

## too [tu] 副 ①也 ②太

① I like roses, *too*.
　我也喜歡玫瑰花。
② The shirt is *too* big for him.
　那襯衫他穿太大了。

### too...to... 太……而不能……

Lucy is *too* short *to* reach the kite on the shelf.
露西太矮了，拿不到架子上的風箏。

### tool [tul] 名 工具

There are many kinds of *tools*.
有許多種工具。

## tooth [tuθ] 名 牙齒

We should clean our *teeth* every morning.
我們每天早晨都得刷牙。
toothbrush 牙刷; toothpaste 牙膏;
toothpick 牙籤; toothache 牙痛

### top [tɑp] 名 ①頂點，頂端 ②陀螺

① A flag is flying on the *top* of the hill.
　山頂上飄揚著一面旗幟。
② Can you spin a *top*?
　你會轉陀螺嗎？

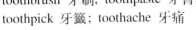

**torch** [tɔrtʃ] 名 手電筒

Where's your *torch*?

你的手電筒在哪裏?

**tortoise** ['tɔrtəs,'tɔrtɪs] 名 龜

A *tortoise* moves very slowly.

龜爬得很慢。

**T**

**total** ['totl] 名 總共的，全部的

What's the *total* number of people coming tomorrow?

明天要來的人員總數是多少?

**touch** [tʌtʃ] 動 觸，摸

Tom *touched* his head.

湯姆摸了摸他的頭。

**tourist** ['turɪst] 名 旅行者，遊客

This *tourist* comes from Taiwan.

這名遊客來自臺灣。

**toward(s)** [tord(z),tɔrd(z),tə'wɔd(z)] 介 朝，向

Betty ran *towards* her mother.

貝蒂向她媽媽跑去。

**towel** ['tau(ə)l] 名 毛巾

Jack is drying himself with a bath *towel*.

傑克用浴巾擦乾身體。

**tower** ['tauɚ,taur] 名 塔

The *tower* is ninety feet high.

這座塔高 90 英呎。

**town** [taun] 名 城鎮

They don't live in a *town*. They live in a city.

他們不住在小鎮上,住在城裏。

**toy** [tɔɪ] 名 玩具

The *toy* is very interesting.

這個玩具非常有趣。

215

**tractor** ['træktɚ] 名 拖拉機；牽引車

    In a city, we seldom see a *tractor*.

    在城市裏，我們很少看見拖拉機。

**traffic** ['træfɪk] 名 交通

    I got stuck in *traffic* yesterday.

    昨天我碰上交通堵塞。

    traffic-light 紅綠燈；traffic-jam 交通阻塞

**train** [tren] 名 火車

    Are you going to Taichung by *train?*

    你們將搭火車去台中嗎？

**trap** [træp] 名 陷阱

    The wolf dropped into the *trap*.

    狼掉進陷阱裏去了。

**travel** ['trævl̩] 動 旅遊，旅行

    I want to *travel* around the world.

    我想去周遊世界。

**treat** [trit] 動 對待，招待

    Don't *treat* the children like this.

    不要這樣對待孩子。

**tree** [tri] 名 樹

    There are a lot of fruit *trees* at our school.

    我們校園裏有許多水果樹。

**trick** [trɪk] 名 詭計

    Tom played a *trick* on Mike.

    湯姆捉弄了邁克。

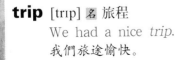

**trip** [trɪp] 名 旅程

    We had a nice *trip*.

    我們旅途愉快。

**trouble** ['trʌbl̩] 名 ①困難　②麻煩

① What's the *trouble*, John?

約翰，出了什麼事？

② I'm sorry to cause you so much *trouble*.

對不起，給你添了這麼多麻煩。

**trousers** ['trɑuzɚz] 名 褲子

Whose *trousers* is Sandy wearing?

桑迪穿的是誰的褲子？

**truant** ['tr(ɪ)uənt] 名 逃學者

Tom said he didn't play *truant*.

湯姆說他沒有逃學。

**truck** [trʌk] 名 卡車

This is Jim's toy *truck*.

這是吉姆的玩具卡車。

**true** [tr(ɪ)u] 形 真實的，確實的

It's *true* that the earth is round.

地球確實是圓的。

**trunk** [trʌŋk] 名 ①樹幹　②象鼻子

①The branches grow from the *trunk*.

樹枝長在樹幹上。

② The elephant lift the tree with its *trunk*.

象用鼻子舉起了樹。

**trust** [trʌst] 動 信任

Do you *trust* me?

你信任我嗎？

**truth** [tr(ɪ)uθ] 名 事實，真相

Tell the *truth*.

要說真話。

**try** [traɪ] 動 試，嘗試

*Try* to be here on time.

盡量準時到這兒。

*Try* on this dress.

試穿一下這件裙子。

**tube** [tjub,t(ɪ)ub] 名 軟管

There is a *tube* of toothpaste and a toothbrush in the glass.

玻璃杯裏有一罐牙膏和一隻牙刷。

**Tuesday** ['tjuzdɪ,'t(ɪ)uzdɪ] 名 星期二

The library is closed on *Tuesday* afternoon.

周二下午圖書館不開門。

**tunnel** ['tʌnl̩] 名 隧道

The train went through several *tunnels*.

火車穿過好幾條隧道。

**turkey** ['tɜkɪ] 名 火雞

They have *turkeys* for Thanksgiving dinner.

他們在感恩節的晚宴上吃火雞。

**turn** [tɜn] 動 轉，旋轉

*Turn* the handle.

轉動門把。

名 輪流，順序

Whose *turn* is it?

輪到誰了？

**turtle** ['tɜtl̩] 名 海龜

A *turtle* lives in the sea.

海龜生活在海裏。

**twelve** ['twɛlv] 數 十二

There are *twelve* inches in a foot.

1 英呎等於 12 英吋。

**twenty** ['twɛntɪ] 數 二十
Let's count to *twenty* in English.
讓我們用英語數到二十。

**twice** [twaɪs] 副 兩次，兩倍
Brush your teeth *twice* a day.
一天刷兩次牙。

**twin** [twɪn] 名 雙胞胎之一
They are *twins*.
他們是雙胞胎。

**two** [tu] 數 二
Where are the *two* boys going?
這兩個男孩要去哪裏?

**type** [taɪp] 動 打字
Jane can *type*.
珍會打字。
typewriter 打字機
typist 打字員

# U

**UFO** [juɛfo] 名 不明飛行物

I heard about *UFO*, but I haven't seen any.

我聽說過不明飛行物，但我從來沒有見過。

**ugly** ['ʌglɪ] 形 醜陋的

This girl looks *ugly*, but she's warm-hearted.

這個姑娘雖相貌醜陋，但心地善良。

反 beautiful 美麗的

**umbrella** [ʌm'brɛlə] 名 雨傘

Jim holds a large *umbrella*.

吉姆撐著一把大雨傘。

**uncle** ['ʌŋkl] 名 叔叔，伯伯，舅舅

My *uncle* is as tall as I am.

我的叔叔和我一樣高。

**under** ['ʌndɚ] 介 在……之下

There isn't a boat *under* the bridge.

橋下沒有一隻船。

反 over 在……之上

**understand** [ʌndɚ'stænd] 動 明白，理解

Do you *understand* me?

你明白我說的話嗎？

**uniform** ['junə,fɔrm] 名 制服
Their school *uniforms* are very nice.
他們的校服非常好看。

**unlucky** [ʌn'lʌkɪ] 形 不幸的，倒霉的
Today is Sandy's *unlucky* day.
今天是桑迪倒霉的日子。
反 lucky 幸運的

**untidy** [ʌn'taɪdɪ] 形 不整潔的，零亂的
The room looks very *untidy*.
這房間看起來非常亂。

**until** [ən'tɪl] 介 連 直至
Don't leave *until* I arrive.
在我到達之前不要離開。
Nothing happened *until* 5 o'clock.
5點以前沒發生任何事情。

**unusual** [ʌn'juʒʊ(ə)l, ʌn'juʒəl] 形 不尋常的
Dick showed Sandy some *unusual* hats.
迪克給桑迪看了一些不同尋常的帽子。
反 usual 通常的

**up** [ʌp] 副 在高處，向高處
The kite is *up* in the tree.
風箏掛在樹上。

介 上，向上
Mike will go *up* the hill tomorrow.
邁克明天將去登山。
反 down 在下方，向下

**upside down** 倒立地
Sandy, Tom and Billy can all
stand *upside down*.
桑迪，湯姆和比利都會倒立。

# upstairs [ʌpˈstɛrz] 副 在樓上的，在樓上
The bedrooms are *upstairs*.
卧室在樓上。
Please go *upstairs*.
請上樓。

## use [jus] 動 使用
If you don't *use* your English, you'll forget it.
如果你不使用所學的英語，你將會忘掉。

名 用途，用處
It's no *use* pretending that you didn't know.
假裝你不知道是沒有用的。

## useful [ˈjusfəl] 形 有用的

## useless [ˈjuslɪs] 形 沒用的
In the desert a camel is *useful*
and a horse is *useless*.
在沙漠中駱駝是有用的，而馬是沒有用的。

## usually [ˈjuʒʊ(ə)l, ˈjuʒəl] 副 通常
The pupils *usually* go to bed at 9:10 at night.
學生們通常在晚上 9 點 10 分上床睡覺。

**V v**

**vacation** [veˈkeʃən; vəˈkeʃən] 名 假期

Their summer *vacation* started.

他們的暑期開始了。

同 vocation 休假

winter vacation 寒假

**vacuum** [ˈvækjʊəm] 名 真空

**vacuum cleaner** 吸塵器

She's cleaning the carpet with the *vacuum cleaner*.

她正在用吸塵器清潔地毯。

**valley** [ˈvælɪ] 名 山谷

The *valley* is deep.

這個山谷很深。

**value** [ˈvæljʊ] 名 價值，價格

The *value* of a color TV is about ten thousand dollars.

一臺彩色電視的價格大約 10000 元。

**vase** [ves, vez] 名 花瓶

The flowers in the *vase* are plastic.

花瓶裏的花是塑膠花。

**vegetable** ['vɛdʒ(ə)təbl] 名 蔬菜

Farmers plant *vegetables* in their fields.
農民們在田地裏種植蔬菜。

**V**

**very** ['vɛrɪ] 副 非常，很

The stories are *very* interesting.
這些故事非常有趣。

**vest** [vɛst] 名 背心

Pupils aren't allowed to wear vests in
the classroom.
學生們在教室裏不允許穿背心。

**vet** [vɛt] 名 獸醫

The *vet* is checking the sick dog.
獸醫正在給那隻生病的狗做檢查。

**video** ['vɪdɪ‚o] 名 影像

Peter is watching the *video*.
彼得在看影像。
videotape　影像帶
videotape recorder　錄影機

**village** ['vɪlɪdʒ] 名 村莊

He's from a poor *village*.
他來自一個貧窮的山村。

**violin** [‚vaɪə'lɪn] 名 小提琴

A *violin* has four strings.
小提琴有四根弦。

**visit** ['vɪzɪt] 動 訪問，拜訪

She *visited* her grandma at the
hospital today.
今天，她去醫院探望了她的祖母。

**visitor** ['vɪzɪtɚ] 名 訪問者，拜訪者

### voice [vɔɪs] 名 聲音

Answer the questions in a loud *voice*.
大聲回答問題。

### volcano [val'keno] 名 火山

This is an active *volcano*.
這是一座活火山。

**V**

### volleyball ['vɑlɪˌbɔl] 名 排球

The children are playing *volleyball*.
孩子們在打排球。

### vote [vot] 動 選舉，投票

Our class will *vote* for monitor tomorrow.
我們班明天投票選班長。

### waist [west] 名 腰，腰部
Betty has a 24-inch *waist*.
貝蒂的腰圍是 24 英吋。

### wait [wet] 動 等待
Sandy and Sue are *waiting* for their teacher.
桑迪和蘇正在等他們的老師。

### wake [wek] 動 叫醒，醒
*Wake* up! It's eight thirty.
醒醒! 已經八點半了。

### walk [wɔk] 動 行走，步行
Let's *walk* to school today!
今天，我們走著去學校吧!

名 步行，散步
Let's take a *walk* by the river!
讓我們去河邊散散步吧!

### wall [wɔl] 名 牆
It's wrong to draw on the *wall*.
在牆上亂畫是不道德的。
the Great Wall　長城

**wallet** ['wɑlɪt, 'wɔlɪt] 名 錢包、皮夾

Diana put one hundred dollars in her *wallet*.

戴安娜往錢包裏裝了一百元。

**wand** [wɑnd] 名 杖，棍

The fairy had a magic *wand*.

仙女有一根魔杖。

**W**

**want** [wɑnt, wɔnt] 動 要，想要

Helen *wants* to buy a pair of sun-glasses.

海倫想買一副太陽鏡。

**war** [wɔr] 名 戰爭

We all hope for peace and hate *war*.

我們都向往和平，憎惡戰爭。

**wardrobe** ['wɔrd,rob] 名 衣櫃

Is my blouse in the *wardrobe*?

我的罩衫在衣櫃裏嗎?

**warm** [wɔrm] 形 溫暖的

Come and get *warm* by the fire.

過來烤烤火暖和暖和。

**wash** [wɑʃ, wɔʃ] 動 洗，清洗

*Wash* your hands before you eat.

吃飯前你要先洗手。

wash basin   洗臉盆

washing machine   洗衣機

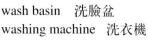

**waste** [west] 動 浪費

Don't *waste* the water.

別浪費水。

反   save 節約

wastepaper 廢紙

wastepaper basket 廢紙簍，廢物箱

**227**

## watch [wɑtʃ, wɔtʃ] 動 注視，觀看

Tom is *watching* TV.

湯姆正在看電視。

名 手錶

My *watch* is five minutes faster.

我的錶快五分鐘。

## water ['wɔtɚ, 'wɑtɚ] 名 水

We must drink *water* every day.

我們每天必須喝水。

動 澆水

Mary is *watering* her flowers.

瑪麗在給她的花澆水。

## wave [wev] 動 揮手

They *waved* goodbye to each other.

他們揮手告別。

## way [we] 名 ①道路 ②方法

① This is the *way* to the post office.

這是通往郵局的路。

② Can you think of another *way*?

你能想出別的辦法嗎?

## we [wi, 弱 wɪ] 代 我們

*We*'d like to see it for ourselves.

我們想親自去看看。

Show *us* the map.

讓我們看一下地圖。

*Our* map is in the classroom.

我們的地圖在教室裏。

The big classroom is *ours*.

那個大教室是我們的。

## weak [wik] 形 虛弱的

He is too *weak* to walk a long way.

他身體太虛弱不能走太遠。

反 strong 強壯的

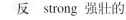

### wear [wɛr,wær] 動 穿，戴

Girls *wear* dresses and boys wear shorts.
女孩子穿裙子，男孩子穿短褲。

### weather ['wɛðɚ] 名 天氣

We had good *weather* on our vacation.
我們的假期趕上了好天氣。

# Wednesday ['wɛnzdɪ] 名 星期三

Today is *Wednesday*, isn't it?
今天是星期三，對嗎？

# weed [wid] 名 雜草

The farmer is pulling up the
*weeds* in the field.
那個農民正在拔田地裏的雜草。

# week [wik] 名 星期

A *week* has seven days.
一星期有 7 天。
weekday 周一到周六的任何一天
weekend 周末，星期六和星期天

### weigh [we] 動 稱……重量

Jane is *weighing* herself on the scale.
珍正在磅稱上稱體重。

### weight [wet] 名 重量

They are the same *weight*.
他們體重相等。

# welcome ['wɛlkəm] 嘆 歡迎

*Welcome* to Taiwan!
歡迎到台灣來！
形 受歡迎的，令人愉快的
"Thank you for your help."
"謝謝你的幫助。"
"You are *welcome*."
"別客氣(不用謝)。"

# well [wɛl] 副 好

Mr. White speaks Chinese *well*.
懷特先生中文講得很好。

as *well* 也

形 好的、健康的
Sue didn't feel *well* this morning.
今天早上蘇感覺到不舒服。

名 井
In the poor village, people draw water from the old *well*.
在這個貧窮的村子裏，人們從那口老井裏打水。

歎 哦，唔，哎呀
*Well*, let's go and see.
哦，我們去看看吧。

## west [wɛst] 名 西，西部

The sun sets in the *west*.
太陽在西方落下。

反 east 東，東方

## wet [wɛt] 形 濕的

Lucy is *wet* through.
露茜渾身上下都濕透了。

反 dry 乾的

# whale [hwel] 名 鯨

A *whale* isn't a kind of fish.
鯨不是魚。

# what [hwɑt,弱 wət] 代 什麼

*What* is she looking at?
她正在看什麼？

*What*'s this in English?
這個（東西）用英語怎麼説？

# wheel [hwil] 名 車輪，輪子

A *wheel* is rolling down the hill.
一個輪子從小山上滾下來了。

**when** [hwɛn] 副 什麼時候

*When* will your parents come back?
你父母什麼時候回來？

連 當……時候
We cheered *when* we got to the peak.
當到達山頂時，我們歡呼起來。

**where** [hwɛr,hwær] 副 去哪裏，在哪裏

*Where* are you going, Tom?
湯姆，你去哪裏？

**which** [hwɪtʃ] 代 哪一個，哪些

*Which* one do you want?
你想要哪一個？

**while** [hwaɪl] 連 當……時候，在……期間

Billy fell asleep *while* he was taking
the test.
比利在考試時睡著了。

**whisper** ['hwɪspɚ] 動 低聲，耳語

Dick *whispered* something to Jane.
迪克小聲地對珍說話。

**whistle** ['hwɪsl] 名 口哨

Mike is blowing a *whistle*.
邁克在吹哨子。

**white** [hwaɪt] 形 白色的

The walls of our classroom are *white*.
我們教室的牆是白色的。
反 black 黑色的

**who** [hu] 代 誰

*Who* are the young men?
那些年輕人是誰？

**whole** [hol,hʊl] 形 整個的，全部的
David stayed at home for a *whole* day.
大衛在家裏待了一整天。

**whose** [huz] 代 誰的
*Whose* pen is this?
這枝鋼筆是誰的？

**why** [hwaɪ,弱 waɪ] 副 為什麼
*Why* were you late?
你為什麼遲到了？

**wide** [waɪd] 形 寬廣的，寬闊的
How *wide* is the bridge!
這座橋多寬啊!
反 narrow 窄的

**wife** [waɪf] 名 妻子
She's a good *wife* and mother.
她是一位賢妻良母。

**wild** [waɪld] 形 野生的
There are many *wild* animals in the forest.
森林裏住著許多野生動物。

**will** [wɪl,弱 wəl,l] 助動 ①願，要　②可能
① I *will* do my best to help you.
　我願盡力幫助你。
② This *will* do if there's nothing better.
　如果沒有更好的這個也行。

**win** [wɪn] 動 獲勝，贏
Who do you think will *win*?
你認為誰將獲勝?
winner 獲勝者

**wind** [wɪnd] 名 風
The *wind* blew Mary's hat away.
風把瑪麗的帽子吹跑了。

**window** ['wɪndo] 名 窗戶
Open the *window*, please.
請把窗戶開大一點。

**windy** ['wɪndɪ] 形 大風的，有風的
It's *windy* today.
今天有風。

W

**wing** [wɪŋ] 名 翅膀
Birds fly with two *wing*s.
鳥用雙翅飛翔。

**winter** ['wɪntɚ] 名 冬天，冬季
It's very cold in the *winter*.
冬天非常冷。

**wire** [waɪr] 名 金屬線
*Wire*s carry electricity.
金屬線能導電。

**wish** [wɪʃ] 動 ①祝願　②希望
① I *wish* you good luck!
祝你好運!
② Jim *wishes* he could fly to the moon.
吉姆希望他能飛到月球上去。

**witch** [wɪtʃ] 名 巫婆，女巫
The *witch* is very bad.
這個巫婆非常惡毒。

**with** [wɪð,wɪθ] 介 ①和　②用
① Helen went shopping *with* her mother.
海倫和媽媽一起去買東西。
② The children are drawing *with* color pencils.
孩子們在用彩色筆畫畫。

**without** [wɪð'aʊt,wɪθ'aʊt] 介副 沒有
I came out *without* any money.
我沒帶錢就出來了。

**wolf** [wʊlf] 名 狼

Do you know the story
of the *wolf* and the lamb?
你知道狼和小羊的故事嗎？

**woman** ['wʊmən] 名 婦女，女人

There is a woman sitting on the chair.
椅子上坐著一個女人。

**wonder** ['wʌndə] 名 奇蹟

What are the seven *wonders* of the world?
世界七大奇蹟是什麼？

**wonderful** ['wʌndəfəl] 形 奇妙的，令人驚奇的

It's a *wonderful* place.
那是一個奇妙的地方。

**wood** [wʊd] 名 木頭，木材

Our desks and chairs are all made of *wood*.
我們的課桌椅都是由木頭製成的。

**wool** [wʊl] 名 羊毛，毛線

My sweater is made of *wool*.
我的毛衣是由毛線織成的。

**word** [wɜd] 名 字，詞

How many *words* have you learned?
你們已經學了多少個單字了？

**work** [wɜk] 動 名 工作

David *works* in an office. Every day he must do a lot of work.
大衛在一間辦公室工作，每天他必須處理許多工作。
反 rest 休息
worker 工人
workshop 工廠

**world** [wɜld] 名 世界

This is a map of the *world*.
這是一張世界地圖。

**worm** [wɜm] 名 蟲子

Hens and cocks like *worms*.
母鷄和公鷄喜歡吃蟲子。
a silkworm　蠶
an earthworm　蚯蚓

**W**

**worry** ['wɜɪ] 動 擔心，擔憂

Don't *worry* about him!
不要替他擔心。

**would** [wʊd,弱 wəd,d] 助動 要，願意

*Would* you like some ice cream?
你想要些冰淇淋嗎?

**wrap** [ræp] 動 包，裹

Sue *wraps* the box up with colored paper.
蘇用色紙把盒子包起來。

**wrist** [rɪst] 名 手腕

Jim wears a new watch on his *wrist*.
吉姆手腕上戴了一隻新錶。

**write** [raɪt] 動 寫

*Write* your name on the paper first.
首先在試卷上寫上名字。

**wrong** [rɔŋ] 形 ①錯誤的，不正確的　②失常的

① That's where you are *wrong*.
那是你的錯誤所在。
反　right 正常的
② What's *wrong* with you?
你怎麼啦?

**X ray** ['ɛks're'] 名 X射線，X光照片

The doctor took an *X ray* of Mike's lungs.
醫生拍了一張邁克肺臟的X光片。

**xylophone** ['zaɪlə,fon, 'zɪl,fon] 名 木琴

We use small wooden hammers
to play the *xylophone*.
我們用小木槌來演奏木琴。

**Y**

**yard** [jɑrd] 名 ①院子 ②碼

The children are playing in the *yard*.

孩子們正在院裏玩。

**yawn** [jɔn] 動 打哈欠

I *yawn* when I'm tired.

我睏的時候總打哈欠。

**year** [jɪr] 名 年

There are 365 days in a *year*.

一年有 365 天。

Are you eleven *years* old?

你是 11 歲嗎?

**yell** [jɛl] 動 叫喊, 喊叫

He *yells* at the naughty boys.

他朝那些頑皮的男孩子喊叫。

**yellow** ['jɛlo] 形 黃色的

His raincoat is *yellow*.

What about yours?

他的雨衣是黃色的, 你的呢?

**yes** [jɛs] 副 是, 是的

Just answer *yes* or no.

只需回答是與不是。

**yesterday** ['jɛstədɪ, 'jɛstə·de] 名副 昨天

Yesterday was July 3rd.

昨天是 7 月 3 日。

I got up early yesterday morning.

我昨天早上起得很早。

**yet** [jɛt] 副 到此時，至今

I haven't finished my work yet.

我還沒有完成我的工作。

Have you received a letter from him yet?

你收到過他的來信嗎?

**yolk** [jok, jolk] 名 蛋黃

Some pupils left the yolks on the table.

一些學生把蛋黃留在了桌子上。

**you** [ju, 弱 jʊ, jə] 代 你，你們

You are wrong.

你錯了。

Let me help you.

讓我來幫你。

Pass me your paper.

把你的試卷遞給我。

Now you can do it by yourself.

現在你可以自己做了。

**young** [jʌŋ] 形 年輕的

The young man is a mailman.

那個年輕人是郵差。

反 old 年老的

**Yo-Yo** ['jo,jo] 名 溜溜球

Lucy is playing with a Yo-Yo.

露西在玩溜溜球。

# Z z

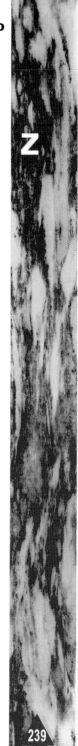

Z

**zebra** ['zɪbrə] 名 斑馬
"It's a *zebra*."
"這是匹斑馬。"
a zebra crossing 斑馬線

**zero** ['zɪro,'ziro] 名 零
Dick got a *zero* on his last math test.
迪克在上次數學測驗中得了零分。

**zip** [zɪp] 名 拉鏈
My *zip* is broken.
我的拉鏈壞了。

**zoo** [zu] 名 動物園
The children enjoy going to the *zoo*.
孩子們喜歡去那個動物園。

# 數、時間和日期

## （一）基數

| | | | |
|---|---|---|---|
| 1 | one | 18 | eighteen |
| 2 | two | 19 | nineteen |
| 3 | three | 20 | twenty |
| 4 | four | 21 | twenty-one |
| 5 | five | 22 | twenty-two |
| 6 | six | 23 | twenty three |
| 7 | seven | 30 | thirty |
| 8 | eight | 40 | forty |
| 9 | nine | 50 | fifty |
| 10 | ten | 60 | sixty |
| 11 | eleven | 70 | seventy |
| 12 | twelve | 80 | eighty |
| 13 | thirteen | 90 | ninety |
| 14 | fourteen | 100 | one hundred |
| 15 | fifteen | 1,000 | one thousand |
| 16 | sixteen | 10,000 | ten thousand |
| 17 | seventeen | | |

## 二 序數

| 第一 | the first（1st） |
| 第二 | the second（2nd） |
| 第三 | the third（3rd） |
| 第四 | the fourth（4th） |
| 第五 | the fifth（5th） |
| 第六 | the sixth（6th） |
| 第七 | the seventh（7th） |
| 第八 | the eighth（8th） |
| 第九 | the ninth（9th） |
| 第十 | the tenth（10th） |
| 第十一 | the eleventh（11th） |
| 第十二 | the twelfth（12th） |
| 第十三 | the thirteenth（13th） |
| 第十四 | the fourteenth（14th） |
| 第十五 | the fifteenth（15th） |
| 第十六 | the sixteenth（16th） |
| 第十七 | the seventeenth（17th） |
| 第十八 | the eighteenth（18th） |
| 第十九 | the nineteenth（19th） |
| 第二十 | the twentieth（20th） |
| 第二十一 | the twenty-first（21st） |
| 第二十二 | the twenty-second（22nd） |
| 第二十三 | the twenty-third（23rd） |
| 第二十四 | the twenty-fourth（24th） |
| 第二十五 | the twenty-fifth（25th） |
| 第三十 | the thirtieth（30th） |
| 第四十 | the fourtieth（40th） |

## （三）時間

| | |
|---|---|
| 二分鐘 | two minutes |
| 三個小時 | three hours |
| 約四個小時 | about four hours |
| 正好五個小時 | just five hours |
| 現在 | now |
| 中午 | noon |
| 下午六點十分 | six ten p.m. |
| 凌晨二點半 | two thirty a.m. |
| 今天 | today |
| 明天 | tomorrow |
| 昨天 | yesterday |
| 今天早晨 | this morning |
| 明天早晨 | tomorrow morning |
| 今天下午 | this afternoon |
| 明天下午 | tomorrow afternoon |
| 昨天下午 | yesterday afternoon |

## （四）星期，四季

| | |
|---|---|
| 這周 | this week |
| 下周 | next week |
| 上周 | last week |
| 星期日 | Sunday |
| 星期一 | Monday |
| 星期二 | Tuesday |
| 星期三 | Wednesday |
| 星期四 | Thursday |

| | |
|---|---|
| 星期五 | Friday |
| 星期六 | Saturday |
| 春 | spring |
| 夏 | summer |
| 秋 | autumn |
| 冬 | winter |
| 早春 | early spring |
| 晚秋 | late autumn |

## 五 月

| | |
|---|---|
| 一月 | January |
| 二月 | February |
| 三月 | March |
| 四月 | April |
| 五月 | May |
| 六月 | June |
| 七月 | July |
| 八月 | August |
| 九月 | September |
| 十月 | October |
| 十一月 | November |
| 十二月 | December |
| 下個月 | next month |
| 上個月 | last month |
| 四月上旬 | early April |
| 四月中旬 | mid April |
| 四月下旬 | late April |
| 四月末 | end of April |

243

# 動詞三態

## (一) 第三人稱的動詞現在式

❏ 直接加 "s" 的動詞:

(當主詞為第三人稱單數時，其動詞必以 "s" 結尾)

例： 〔-z〕 〔-s〕

play-plays ask-asks

love-loves help-helps

❏ 接 "es" 的動詞:

(以 -s,-ch,-sh 結束的動詞，如遇主詞為第三人稱時，則加上 "es")

例： 〔-iz〕

pass-passes wash-washes

❏ 字尾是子音 + "y" 形式的動詞:

(將 y 去掉，以 ies 取代)

例： carry-carries

study-studies

## (二) 過去式與過去分詞

❏ 大部分動詞的過去式都直接在字尾加 "ed"

例： 〔-d〕 〔-t〕

play-played pass-passed

start-started

❏ 以 "e" 結尾的動詞，過去式直接加 "d"

例： 〔-d〕 〔-t〕

smile-smiled like-liked

❑(短母音) + (以子音結束)的動詞, 它的過去式要重覆字尾再加 "ed"

例：stop-stopped

❑(子音) + (以"y"結束)的動詞, 它的過去式要去掉"y"加"ied"

例：carry-carried　　　　cry-cried

## 三 現在式 -ing

❑大部分動詞的現在式都直接在字尾加"ing"

例：start-starting

❑以"e"結尾的動詞, 現在式去掉"e"直接加"ing"

例：make-making

❑(短母音) + (以子音結束)的動詞, 它的現在式要重覆字尾再加 "ing"

例：run-running　　　　swim-swimming

❑以"ie"結尾的動詞, 現在式去掉"ie"直接加"ying"

例：die-dying　　　　lie-lying

附 錄 三

# 名詞的各種複數形式

(一) 直接在字尾加上 "s"

[-z]

eye-eyes
flower-flowers
holiday-holidays
hour-hours
letter-letters
picture-pictures
star-stars
tree-trees
uncle-uncles
year-years

[-dz]

bird-birds
cloud-clouds
food-foods
friend-friends
ground-grounds
hand-hands
head-heads
second-seconds
third-thirds

[-s]

book-books
cup-cups
desk-desks
help-helps
lake-lakes
month-months
park-parks
shop-shops
thank-thanks
word-words

[-ts]

aunt-aunts
boat-boats
cut-cuts
fruit-fruits
minute-minutes
night-nights
street-streets
student-students

[-iz]

face-faces
nose-noses
page-pages
rose-roses
village-villages

(二) 凡字尾是 "-s,-x,-ch" 的名詞，其複數形式則是加上 "es"

[-iz]

box-boxes
dish-dishes
bus-buses

lunch-lunches
class-classes

（三）以"y"結尾的名詞，其複數形式去掉"y"直接加"ｉes"

[-z]

| | |
|---|---|
| city-cities | library-libraries |
| country-countries | story-stories |
| cry-cries | study-studies |
| dictionary-dictionaries | try-tries |
| family-families | ☆(例外) boy-boys |

（四）凡字尾以"o"結尾的名詞複數形式加"s"，"es"均可

[-z]

| | |
|---|---|
| piano-pianos | radio-radios |
| potato-potatoes | |

（五）以"f"爲字尾的名詞其複數形式為去掉"f"，加"ves"。

[-vz]

| | |
|---|---|
| half-halves | leaf-leaves |
| knife-knives | ☆(例外)：roof-roofs |

（六）特殊的名詞複數形式

不規則複數形：

| | |
|---|---|
| foot-feet | woman-women |
| man-men | child-children |
| mouse-mice | ox-oxen |
| tooth-teeth | |

單複數同形：

Chinese-Chinese

sheep-sheep

附 錄 四

# 形容詞、副詞的比較級與最高級

## (一) 一般用法，也是最常用的是在字尾直接加 "er"，"est"

| 一般級 | 比較級 | 最高級 |
| --- | --- | --- |
| cold | colder | coldest |
| cool | cooler | coolest |
| dark | darker | darkest |
| fast | faster | fastest |
| hard | harder | hardest |
| high | higher | highest |
| long | longer | longest |
| near | nearer | nearest |
| short | shorter | shortest |
| soon | sooner | soonest |
| tall | taller | tallest |
| young | younger | youngest |

## (二) 若字尾是 "e" 的話則直接加上 "r"，"st"

| 一般級 | 比較級 | 最高級 |
| --- | --- | --- |
| close | closer | closest |
| fine | finer | finest |
| large | larger | largest |
| nice | nicer | nicest |

## (三) 若字尾是 "y" 的話則去掉，直接加上 "ier"，"iest"

| 一般級 | 比較級 | 最高級 |
| --- | --- | --- |
| busy | busier | busiest |
| early | earlier | earliest |
| easy | easier | easiest |
| happy | happier | happiest |
| pretty | prettier | prettiest |

(四) 若形容詞(或副詞)的倒數二字是短母音＋子音字尾，則重覆最後一個字母再加 "er","est"

| 一般級 | 比較級 | 最高級 |
|--------|--------|--------|
| big | bigger | biggest |
| thin | thinner | thinnest |
| hot | hotter | hottest |

(五) 形容詞(或副詞)前加 "more", "most" 的例子：

| 一般級 | 比較級 | 最高級 |
|--------|--------|--------|
| careful | more careful | most careful |
| slowly | more slowly | most slowly |
| interesting | more interesting | most interesting |

(六) 不規則的變化：

| 一般級 | 比較級 | 最高級 |
|--------|--------|--------|
| good(well) | better | best |
| bad(ill) | worse | worst |
| little | less | least |
| many(much) | more | most |
| far | farther | farthest |
|  | further | furthest |
| late | later | latest |
|  | latter | last |
| old | older | oldest |
|  | elder | eldest |

249

# 不規則動詞變化

| 現在式 | 過去式 | 過去分詞 | -ing 形 |
|---|---|---|---|
| am(be) 是 | was | been | being |
| are(be) 是 | were | been | being |
| awake 醒著 | awoke | awoke | awaking |
| | awaked | awaked | |
| be 是 | was,were | been | being |
| bear 生 | bore | borne,born | bearing |
| become 變成…… | became | become | becoming |
| begin 開始 | began | begun | beginning |
| bite 咬 | bit | bitten, | biting |
| break 打破 | broke | broken | breaking |
| bring 帶…… | brought | brought | bringing |
| burn 燃燒 | burned,burnt | burned,burnt | burning |
| buy 買…… | bought | bought | buying |
| can 可能 | could | | |
| catch 捉到 | caught | caught | catching |
| come 來 | came | come | coming |
| cut 切 | cut | cut | cutting |
| do,does 做 | did | done | doing |
| draw 畫 | drew | drawn | drawing |
| dream 夢見 | dreamed, dreamt | dreamed, dreamt | dreaming |
| drink 喝 | drank | drunk | drinking |
| drive 駕，駛 | drove | driven | driving |
| eat 吃 | ate | eaten | eating |
| fall 落下 | fell | fallen | falling |
| feed 飼養 | fed | fed | feeding |
| feel 感覺 | felt | felt | feeling |
| fight 打戰 | fought | fought | fighting |
| find 看見…… | found | found | finding |
| fly 飛 | flew | flown | flying |
| forget 忘記 | forgot | forgotten, | forgetting |
| | | forgot | |
| get 拿到 | got | got,gotten | getting |
| give 給…… | gave | given | giving |

| 現在式 | 過去式 | 過去分詞 | -ing 形 |
|---|---|---|---|
| go 去 | went | gone | going |
| grow 長大 | grew | grown | growing |
| have,has 持有…… | had | had | having |
| hear 聽到…… | heard | heard | hearing |
| hide 隱藏 | hid | hidden,hid | hiding |
| hit 打擊 | hit | hit | hitting |
| hold 持 | held | held | holding |
| hurt 傷害 | hurt | hurt | hurting |
| is(be) 是 | was | been | being |
| keep 保持 | kept | kept | keeping |
| know 知道 | knew | known | knowing |
| learn 學習 | learned, learnt | learned, learnt | learning |
| leave 離去 | left | left | leaving |
| lend 借…… | lent | lent | lending |
| let 讓 | let | let | letting |
| lie 躺著 | lay | lain | lying |
| lose 掉…… | lost | lost | losing |
| make 作…… | made | made | making |
| may 可以 | might | | |
| mean 意謂 | meant | meant | meaning |
| meet 相遇 | met | met | meeting |
| mistake 錯誤 | mistook | mistaken | mistaking |
| must 必須…… | (must) | | |
| pay 支付 | paid | paid | paying |
| put 放置 | put | put | putting |
| read 讀 | read | read | reading |
| ride 騎 | rode | ridden | riding |
| ring 鳴 | rang | rung | ringing |
| rise 升起 | rose | risen | rising |
| run 跑 | ran | run | running |
| say 說…… | said | said | saying |
| see 看…… | saw | seen | seeing |
| sell 賣 | sold | sold | selling |
| send 送 | sent | sent | sending |

| 現在式 | 過去式 | 過去分詞 | -ing 形 |
|---|---|---|---|
| set 放置 | set | set | setting |
| shake 動搖 | shook | shaken | shaking |
| shall 將…… | should | | |
| shine 照耀 | shone | shone | shining |
| shoot 射擊 | shot | shot | shooting |
| show 展示 | showed | shown | showing |
| | | showed | |
| shut 閉,關 | shut | shut | shutting |
| sing 歌 | sang | sung | singing |
| sit 坐 | sat | sat | sitting |
| sleep 睡 | slept | slept | sleeping |
| slide 滑 | slid | slid | sliding |
| smell 聞 | smelt | smelt | smelling |
| | smelled | smelled | |
| speak 說 | spoke | spoken | speaking |
| spell 拼 | spelled,spelt | spelled,spelt | spelling |
| spend 花用 | spent | spent | spending |
| stand 站立 | stood | stood | standing |
| strike 擊敲 | struck | struck | striking |
| swim 游泳 | swam | swum | swimming |
| swing 搖擺 | swung | swung | swinging |
| take 取得 | took | taken | taking |
| teach 教 | taught | taught | teaching |
| tell 告訴 | told | told | telling |
| think 想…… | thought | thought | thinking |
| throw 投 | threw | thrown | throwing |
| understand 理解 | understood | understood | understanding |
| wake 醒的 | woke,waked | waked,woken | waking |
| wear 穿 | wore | worn | wearing |
| wet 濕的 | wet,wetted | wet,wetted | wetting |
| will 將…… | would | | |
| win 贏…… | won | won | winning |
| write 寫…… | wrote | written | writing |

# 最基礎最簡單的常用會話語句

★ GOOD MORNING.
早安。

★ HOW ARE YOU?
您好嗎。

FINE, THANK YOU.
很好，謝謝。

★ PLEASE COME IN.
請進。

★ YES.
好的。

★ NO.
不是。

★ THANKS.
謝謝您。

★ YOU ARE WELCOME.
不客氣。

★ SORRY.
對不起。

★ NEVER MIND.
不要緊。

★ EXCUSE ME.
抱歉。

★ WHAT IS YOUR NAME?
請問貴姓？

★ I AM WANG.
我姓王。

★ HOW ARE YOU?
您好？

★ A LITTLE BIT.
一點點。

★ PLEASE REPEAT.
請再說一次。

★ PLEASE SPEAK SLOWLY.
請講慢一點。

★ PLEASE WAIT A MOMENT.
請等一下。

★ PLEASE SIGN HERE.
請簽這裡。

★ DO YOU UNDERSTAND?
您明白嗎？

★ SO IT IS.
原來這樣。

★ SO.
這。

★ THIS WAY PLEASE.
請走這邊。

★ AFTER YOU.
您請先。

★ TAKE CARE.
請留心走。

★ PLEASE SIT DOWN.
請坐。

★ NO CEREMONY.
請別客氣。

★ PLEASE HELP YOURSELF.
請用。

★ HOW IS IT?
如何？

★ WHAT DO YOU NEED?
您要什麼？

★ COFFEE OR MILK?
要咖啡還是牛奶？

★ I WANT BREAD AND MILK.
我要麵包和牛奶。

★ I DON'T NEED.
我不需要。

★ WHAT IS THIS?
這是什麼？

★ WHERE IS THE BANK?
銀行在哪裡？

★ WHERE IS YOUR MOTHER?
令堂在何處？

★ WHERE DO YOU WANT TO GO?
您要去哪兒？

★ WHAT TIME IS IT?
現在幾點？

★ WHAT TIME ARE YOU OFF?
您幾點下班？

★ HOW MUCH?
多少錢？

★ HOW OLD ARE YOU?
你幾歲呢？

★ HOW TO DO IT?
怎麼辦呢？

★ I DON'T KNOW.
我不知道。

★ ARE YOU READY?
您準備好了嗎？

★ QUICKLY!
快點！

★ IT IS SOLD OUT.
賣完了。

★ FULL HOUSE.
客滿。

★ HE JUST LEFT.
他剛剛出去。

★ WHAT IS WRONG?
怎麼了？

★ GOOD-BYE!
再見！

★ COME AGAIN.
請再光臨。

★ HOW ARE YOU?
您好嗎？

★ FINE, AND YOU.
您好。

★ THANK YOU, I AM FINE.
託你的福，我很好。

★ ARE YOU GOING OUT?
要出去嗎？

★ ARE YOU BUYING SOMETHING?
您要買東西嗎？

★ ARE YOU GOING TO WORK?
去上班嗎？

★ IT IS FINE.
真是好天氣。

★ IT IS HOT TODAY.
今天真熱。

★ I AM LEAVING.
我走了。

★ SEE YOU.
您好走。

★ I AM BACK.
我回來了。

★ WELCOME BACK.
你回來了。

★ I HAVE TO GO.
我要走了。

★ AFTER YOU.
請先走。

★ BON VOYAGE!
一路順風！

★ TAKE CARE YOURSELF.
請保重。

★ CONGRATULATION!
恭禧！

★ HAPPY NEW YEAR!
恭賀新禧！

★ YES!
是的！

★ NO!
不是！

★ THANK YOU SO MUCH!
真謝謝了！

★ YOU ARE WELCOME.
不謝。

★ I AM SORRY!
對不起！

★ VERY SORRY.
非常抱歉。

★ SORRY.
對不起。

★ EXCUSE ME.
我失陪一下。

★ MAY BE.
說不定如此。

★ NO WONDER.
原來如此。

★ NEVER MIND.
沒關係。

★ PLEASE DON'T MIND.
請不要介意。

★ I KNOW IT.
我知道。

★ I DON'T KNOW.
我不知道。

★ IS THAT SO?
真的嗎？

★ WONDERFUL!
好棒！

★ AS YOU SAID.
正如你所說。

★ INCREDIABLE.
無法相信。

★ I AGREED.
我贊成。

★ I DON'T AGREED.
我不贊成。

★ IT IS PITIFUL.
好可憐。

★ IT IS REGRETFUL!
真可惜！

★ ANY BODY HERE?
有人在嗎？

★ PLEASE COME IN.
請進。

★ PLEASE WAIT FOR A MOMENT.
請稍等。

★ THIS WAY PLEASE.
請這邊走。

★ SORRY TO BOTHER YOU.
打擾了。

★ HOPE TO MEET YOU AGAIN.
希望能再見面。

★ PLEASE FEEL AT HOME.
請別拘束。

★ TAKE A SIT PLEASE.
請坐。

★ PLEASE START.
開動了。

★ HOPE YOU WILL BE SATISFIED.
希望能令您滿意。

★ WHAT DO YOU DRINK?
要喝些什麼飲料？

★ HOW ABOUT ONE MORE?
再添一碗如何？

★ THANKS FOR YOUR ENTERTAINMENT.
謝謝您的招待。

★ JUST A SIMPLE MEAL.
粗茶淡飯而已。

★ NO CEREMONY.
請別客氣。

★ CAN I BORROW THE LIGHTER.
麻煩借一下火。

★ ARE YOU LEAVING?
要走了嗎？

★ COME AGAIN.
請再來。

★ PLEASE COME AGAIN.
請再來。

★ I SHALL COME MORE OFTEN.
我會常來。

★ LET'S HAVE LUNCH TOGETHER?
一起吃飯好嗎？

★ CAN I LOOK AT THE MENU?
請讓我看菜單。

★ COULD YOU MAKE IT RIGHT AWAY?
能不能馬上好？

★ HOW IS THE TASTE?
味道如何？

★ I HAVE TAKEN ENOUGH.
我已經吃夠了。

★ SEND ME THE BILL.
請算帳。

★ LONG TIME NO SEE.
久違了。

★ NOTHING CHANGE.
還是老樣子。

★ IS IT CONVENIENT?
方便嗎？

★ NOT FEELING WELL.
不怎麼舒服。

★ I HAVE FEVER.
發燒了。

★ MAY I BOTHER YOU?
有事想麻煩一下？

★ WHERE IS THE TOILET?
廁所在哪裡？

★ WHERE IS THE STATION?
車站在哪邊？

★ ANY DISCOUNT?
能不能打折？

★ NO BARGAIN.
不二價。

★ HOW MUCH IS ADMISSION?
門票多少錢？

★ CAN I TAKE PICTURE?
能不能拍照？

★ TODAY IS JUNE TENTH.
今天是六月十號。

★ LAST MONTH WAS MAY.
上個月是五月。

★ TODAY IS WEDNESDAY.
今天是週三。

★ I WANT TO GO TO DEPART-
MENT STORE.
我想去百貨公司。

★ I AM GOING NOWHERE.
我哪兒也不去。

★ I HAVE BEEN TO JAPAN.
我去過日本。

★ I HAVE NOT TAKEN A TRAM.
我沒坐過電車

★ I GAVE MR. LEE A NECK TIE.
我給李先生領帶。

★ THIS WAS GIVEN BY MOTHER.
這是向媽媽要來的。

★ THIS WAS GIVEN BY BROTHER.
這是哥哥給我的。

★ THIS BOOK WAS GIVEN BY
TEACHER.
這書是老師給我的。

★ HOW TO SAY IN ENGLISH?
英語怎麼說？

★ MUST GET UP AT SIX.
六點一定得起來。

★ WILL YOU CLOSE THE WINDOW?
請關窗戶好嗎？

★ PLEASE BRING HERE.
請拿來。

★ PLEASE TAKE AWAY.
請拿去。

★ MAY WE DRINK?
可以喝酒嗎？

★ MAY I SMOKE?
可以抽煙嗎？

★ ARE YOU IN A HURRY?
趕著要嗎？

★ HOW ABOUT GOING TOGETHER?
一齊去好嗎？

★ PLEASE SAY AGAIN.
請再說一次。

★ TIME IS UP.
時間到。

# 單 字 索 引

## A a

## B b

# N n

# O o

# P p

# Q q

# R r

## S s

# T t

## V v

## U u